FATALLY

HAUNTED

ANTHOLOGIES BY SISTERS IN CRIME LA

Murder X13
A Deadly Dozen
Murder on Sunset Boulevard
LAndmarked for Murder
Murder in LA-LA-Land
LAst Exit to Murder
LAdies Night
LAst Resort
Fatally Haunted

SISTERS IN CRIME/LOS ANGELES
PRESENTS

FATALLY
HAUNTED

EDITED BY
RACHEL HOWZELL HALL, SHEILA LOWE
AND LAURIE STEVENS

Introduction by CARA BLACK

Down & Out Books
3959 Van Dyke Rd, Ste. 265
Lutz, FL 33558
www.DownAndOutBooks.com

The characters and events in this book are fictitious. Any similarity to real persons, living or dead, is coincidental and not intended by the author.

Cover design by JT Lindroos

ISBN: 1-948235-80-3
ISBN-13: 978-1-948235-80-8

CONTENTS

INTRODUCTION
Cara Black

We're all acquainted with a version of Los Angeles, the place of dreams, of stardom, originally the city of angels, once a pit stop surrounded by orange groves. Even if you've never visited, the place conjures up images—tinsel town, spider webs of freeways and those lush purple jacaranda trees. This city of seventy-two suburbs as Dorothy Parker called it and in Orson Welles' words a "bright and guilty place." For me, the draw was the Sunset Strip and the L.A. of Raymond Chandler. Chandler's words painted a noir locale, evoked shady low-lifes, tarnished sides of glitz, and sparks of beauty tainted by the past. In Chandler's Los Angeles, "the streets were dark with something more than night."

You could say I joined Sisters in Crime in Los Angeles with some of that clinging in my mind. More for the camaraderie, mean margaritas and talking "shop" in the bar. It's amazing what fellow crime writers talk about in their "natural" habitat; blood spatter patterns, a crooked DA, going on an adverb diet, the wild mountain lions in the San Gabriel mountains, plotting a chase scene in Silver Lake. Talk to crime writers at a bar and be prepared.

INTRODUCTION

These fellow writers' talents abound in the fourteen stories in *Fatally Haunted*, an evocative Sisters in Crime anthology. Loaded with a wide range of tales going from sun-drenched secrets to the shadowy and dark. All noir-themed and haunting. These stories showcase the mystique and menace made famous in films and novels and the Angelenos who live them.

Fatally Haunted immerses us in the authors' gifted take on a city "...discernible only in glimpses," as James Ellroy says. These glimpses are haunted—fatally haunted.

From a missing twin sister in Julie G. Beers' "Shifting Reflections," to a twentieth-century serial killer's bizarre clues in Julia Bricklin's "Auble's Ghost," from "Strands of Time" by Roger Cannon where a ten-year reunion brings murder, and in "The End Justifies the Means" Tony Chiarchiaro explores the age-old question is sweet revenge worth the ultimate toll? In "Tick-Tock" Lisa Ciarfella's story of a woman on the run doing one last heist yet can't outrun her demons, to 1930s' Los Angeles featuring in "The Funnel of Love" by Cyndra Gernet where a carney worker tries to escape the past, B.J. Graf explores the mind of a serial killer who's made a mistake at the crime scene in "Blood Shadows," to "Coincidence" by Mark Hague a light rail engineer suffers *deja vu* from a previous murder committed on the tracks, and the iconic Hollywood sign features a haunted H in A.P. Jamison's "Death of the Hollywood Sign Girl." "Palimpsest" brings an antique dealer in the sights of a man obsessed with a lost treasure by Micheal Kelly, and the first Khmer-American police officer on the LBPD, in Alison McMahan's "King Hanuman" doesn't bargain that a simple arrest will lead to a gang war, to Peter Sexton's "Darkness Keeps Chasing" the worst parent's nightmare comes true when an LAPD detective's daughter is abducted, and back to 1948 when a waitress recognizes the man who left her for dead years earlier in "Resurrection" by Jennifer Younger, and topping it off in Gobind Tanaka's thrilling "Cat Walks into a Bank" a Marine Corps vet suffers

PTSD flashbacks while thwarting a violent bank robbery.

Make yourself a cocktail, turn off the phone, settle back and open *Fatally Haunted*. You'll find the city of angels haunted by devils.

DEATH OF THE HOLLYWOOD SIGN GIRL
A.P. Jamison

Los Angeles looked a lot nicer from atop the massive wood and metal "H" of the Hollywood Sign—I couldn't see the rats or the trash or the broken dreams from here. I had already written my obit. It was safely tucked into my breast pocket, where I knew it would survive the fall.

I, Jake Merriman Sinclair, would be dead very soon.

Dusk had descended on the city of angels and devils. My half-empty bottle of booze was jammed into my blazer pocket. The evening breeze, a bit brisker up here, cut through my clothes, but I felt no pain. My tongue tasted of new whiskey and old coffee.

Hollywood. A place where dreams came true...When the sign was built in 1923 proclaiming this to be Hollywood-land—they were selling lots for a new housing development—and not heralding the siren call of the silver screen.

Nevertheless, the sign had become a beacon of hope to so many like me, dazzled by the big screen dream, that in 1949, the powers-that-be dropped "land" from the end of the sign. Hollywood had officially made her formal debut.

Back in the darkness, I wrestled my cell phone from my pants pocket, thankful for its light. Steadying myself, I scrolled to the email, feeling compelled to read the key bruising words again, even though I now knew them by heart.

"We are passing on your screenplay: *Death of the Hollywood Sign Girl*. The story about a Hollywood starlet who killed herself in the 1930s is old news and not relevant today. We are looking for stud superheroes not sad starlets."

My hand shook. "The starlet," I shouted to the world, "was named Peg Entwistle!" I stared down at the water-challenged bushes clinging to the empty Hollywood hills below me. "The world needs to know the true tragedy of Peg. Her story has to be told so it doesn't happen again."

My sneaker slipped off the sign making the whiskey in my system race around my heart like a three-wheeled go-cart. I quickly found my footing and shouted, "Peg. You had the talent!"

Millicent Lilian "Peg" Entwistle had been a successful New York theater actress who headed to Los Angeles during The Great Depression in hopes of finding film opportunities. The age of talkies had just begun, and my research told me Hollywood was looking for actresses with Broadway experience. Money was tight, so Peg had planned to move in with her Uncle Harold at 2428 Beachwood Canyon just below the Hollywoodland Sign. I could almost see her Uncle's house from my unique "H" vantage point.

"Peg," I yelled. "Can you hear me?"

Once she had arrived in L.A., she was met with one cold rejection after another. Like so many actresses after a big audition, she raced home, sat by the phone and waited and waited and waited for a call that never came. So, on the hot night of

September 16, 1932, drunk and depressed, Peg left her Uncle's house, hiked up to the Hollywoodland Sign, climbed fifty feet up a workman's ladder to the top of the "H"—losing her shoe in the process—and jumped to her death.

She was twenty-four years old.

A few days after Peg died, The Beverly Hills Playhouse called and offered her the lead role...about a woman driven to suicide.

Suddenly, I could smell the scent of gardenia—her favorite perfume—while I imagined how she felt, standing on top of this sign. I am nine years older than Peg was when she died. My screenplay was about her short, sad life. I understood her pain.

My world had become so woeful these last few months. My writer's block was bigger than a small country. The severe designer sofa bed at my friend's house hated me. My last girl-friend broke up with me. Apparently, she needed to find out what she really wanted, and it wasn't me. She ended it right around the time my '98 Ford Fiesta took a permanent siesta, and I had to start taking the bus. I hardly had enough money to keep my beloved golden retriever, Hemingway The Marsh-mallow, in kibbles.

I would rather starve than let The Marshmallow go hungry, so I got a job as a barista. But I was always one step away from being fired for not staying focused on the coffee task at hand. My mind was always elsewhere.

Seeing nighttime L.A. unfold all around me, I sighed. The departing gray clouds and pink sun were spectacular, but the best part was the thousands of tiny lights spread out below between the mountains and moon-filled sky. I took another drink. I needed another drink...I already missed The Marsh-mallow, but I had left him in very loving hands.

It was hard to believe that eleven years ago I had moved out here from the Midwest or the "Middle-West" as F. Scott Fitzgerald liked to say. While I was no Fitzgerald, it comforted me to know that he too had struggled to succeed in Hollywood.

Like F. Scott, my first big love didn't understand that she was supposed to marry me.

Her name was Zoey Reynolds. Head cheerleader. Valedictorian. Dog lover. Beer drinker. Bowling champ.

In high school everyone loved her. Especially me. One day near the end of senior year, when I had been waiting at her locker with a cup of her favorite coffee, she turned the corner and grinned. And, there it was—her right, front tooth, which slightly overlapped her left one. She loved that slight imperfection. I was devoted to it.

"No," Zoey said, her smile disappearing as she opened her locker.

"No, what?" I asked, puzzled. Lately, she had been part ice angel, and part hot, darling demon.

"No, Jake, I won't go to the dance with you. Even if you are prom king."

My shoulders dropped and my stomach followed closely behind.

"You're too nice, Jake. I would ruin you." She slowly exhaled as if suddenly exhausted, and flipped a piece of her champagne-colored hair off of her perfect forehead.

"I'm a lot meaner than you think." I said, crossing my arms to drive home my point.

"No, you are not, but you...are an adorable liar, Jake Sinclair. You are meant to tell beautiful stories. You need to leave home. Leave here. Just go. If you stay, you'll end up like your sad dad who let his dreams die. That would break my heart."

You've just broken mine.

"Jake," Zoey said. "Never give up on your writing dreams. Promise me."

All I could do was nod as she left me standing there, unable to move until I made sure the tepid coffee I was holding met its own depressing end at the bottom of the nearby school trashcan.

* * *

The shrill of police sirens in the distance brought me out of the past. The LAPD were headed my way. It was now illegal to scale this beloved landmark sign. Had someone seen or heard me calling out to Peg?

Should I do a swan dive like she had? Or just jump feet first?

Looking down, I saw a sleek 1930s' Lincoln convertible pull up to the road near the ravine below me. A woman was sitting in the front seat behind an oversized steering wheel.

I blinked. Now I was almost hanging off the "H."

Could that be Peg? She looked just like she did in the photos I had uncovered: the blonde hair in a fashionable, flapper-esque wavy bob, the vintage coat and the classic red lipstick. She leaned over and opened the passenger door.

Then she smiled and waved for me to come down and join her.

The police sirens were almost upon me.

"Come on, Middle-West," she urged in a voice both sultry and sad.

I felt a rush of air...

And then I was sitting in the lush, leather passenger seat of her vintage convertible.

I shut the car door, which was long and heavy, and inhaled her floral perfume. She pressed one of the big rectangular buttons on her AM dashboard radio to change the station.

Mildred Bailey was singing "Wrap Your Troubles in Dreams." I could hear the fabulous scratching sound the turntable needle made on the vinyl record coming through the radio speaker.

"Never give up on your writing dreams. Isn't that what Zoey said?"

Zoey...

Peg continued. "If you had known she would die of cancer six months later, you'd have never left her. Zoey knew that." Peg put her hand on mine. "She's not ready for you to join her."

I tried to process what Peg was saying while her eerie words still echoed in my ears. I closed my eyes while they filled up like a fountain of foggy tears.

"And you need to know that I wasn't a coward," Peg said, softly. "I didn't kill myself."

"You...?" Words escaped me.

"I didn't jump, Jake. I was pushed," she said.

Stunned, my mouth stayed closed for once, but I opened my wet eyes, and she solemnly nodded.

We were now winding our way down the hill just as the police passed us. Orange and purple wildflowers stood in solidarity near a lone sycamore tree on the side of the road. Peg handed me a martini, complete with two olives, in a chilled cocktail glass.

"Who killed you?" I asked, finally finding my words.

"That's what you need to find out," she whispered in the clear diction of a classically trained stage actress. "Start with the note I left."

I glanced back and studied the Hollywood Sign with new intensity as it disappeared in the distance. *Peg had been murdered...*

"Jake...Jake." A deep voice boomed close to my ear.

I turned and realized that I was staring at the nose ring of my twenty-five-year-old hipster, Starbucks manager, Serge, scratching his scruffy sideburn with his hand.

"Snap. Snap. You have customers waiting, dude."

I felt the hot coffee I was making burn my hand through the sides of the cup. I looked down. In the Venti, decaf, dry, extra whip, half-caf, caramel cappuccino I had been spelling out the word "murder" in the foam. I glanced up. The young woman standing before me was tall, tempting and blonde—like some sort of glamorous ghost. She smelled of gardenias.

I now had a lump in my throat as big as the extra whipped cream I added to cover up the word "murder." Handing her the large coffee, I stammered, "Sorry about that."

"No worries," she replied in the voice of a classically trained actress. Then she smiled. Her right, front tooth slightly overlapped her left one. "Thanks for the coffee, and never give up on those daydreams," she said, as she turned on her pointed high-heel and headed for the exit.

My stunned eyes followed her as she disappeared through the door.

Past the sunlit window, I caught a glimpse of the Hollywood Sign in the distance and could almost hear a voice whisper, "Hollywood always loves a murder. Find out who killed me, darling Middle-West. That won't be old news..."

In that twisted twilight moment, I knew I had to go get my beloved Marshmallow right now and honor the promise I had made to Zoey long ago.

It was time to put down the bottle and pick up the pen. Peg hadn't given up; neither should I.

KING HANUMAN
Alison McMahan

Long Beach, CA, 1990

"They say the murder victim was the head of the Jewel Orchid gang." Officer Thavary Keo steered the police cruiser through the now-thinning crowds. Last night's drive-by shooting had led to tonight's anti-immigrant demonstration. After the hot and stressful day, it felt good to drive with the window down and relish the briny night air.

My first demonstration. Lucky it was peaceful.

Her new partner, Officer Carlos Urrieta, looked like a star from a *telenovela*. Thick hair, cropped close to his skull. Curved, elegant eyebrows, athletic build, his eyes golden brown where hers were dark, his skin just a shade lighter than hers. He opened the box of Khmer cakes and studied the contents. When his hand crept into the box, Thavary slapped it away. "Those are for your mother."

"So do you have any inside knowledge on the Jewel Orchid gang?"

Thavary swallowed her irritation. "Just 'cause I was born in Cambodia doesn't mean I'm an expert in Cambodian gangs."

"You get offended too easy, you know that?"

A bead of sweat ran down Thavary's neck, cold on her hot spine. Urrieta was right, but admitting it would lead to a conversation about her past, about her escape, about the refugee camp. And then the part she couldn't bear to think about, about the ones that didn't make it. "What about you? You're Mexican. Do you know anything about the Els-Els?"

Urrieta sat up straight, raised his hand, and declaimed in a gravelly deadpan that exactly mimicked their sergeant's: "The Jewel Orchid gang and the Els-Els each control different parts of Anaheim street. Both want to control all of it. Big fight brewing."

Thavary smiled. "Well, now that Jewel Orchid has lost its leader, maybe they will disband."

"Unless whoever killed the old leader plans to take over."

The CB radio crackled. "Thavary. Officer Keo. Can you hear me?"

"That's my foster mother." Thavary grabbed the mike. "Moms, you know you aren't supposed to use Dad's police scanner."

"I need your help, Thavary! They're taking my car!" Her foster-mother's radio-tinny voice choked with rage.

"You at the center, Moms?"

"Yes, Thavary, please!"

Thavary started the lightbar flashing and did a U-turn.

Urrieta turned on the siren. "Can you give us a description, ma'am? How many?"

"They're all kids! Cambos, all of them! They're going to wreck my car, then what will I do?"

"We'll be right there."

The rec center vaguely resembled a bunker, set in an earth-mound covered with mottled grass. The sun setting into the smog turned the sky behind the center a fiery orange and red.

Thavary slowed and turned her head from side to side, peering at the parked cars.

There. Mom's old gas guzzler. *When I pass my first eval,*

I'm getting her a new one.

A teenager jimmied the door. Smaller kids kept watch.

A heavy feeling spread from her chest to her belly. It was true. All the kids were Khmer.

She and Urrieta jumped out of the cruiser. Thavary chased the one who'd jimmied the door, reached out, and grabbed his shoulder. He wasn't a big kid, but she was just below the minimal five-foot departmental height requirement—waived in her case because they were desperate for Khmer cops.

And the kid could fight. As soon as she grabbed him he whirled around and stabbed at her with the screwdriver.

Thavary blocked the weapon. The kid stepped away expertly, then turned back and slashed at her leg.

He was younger than she'd thought at first. But he had a knowingness to the arch of his eyebrows, craftiness in the light in his eyes, a feral hunger in his crooked teeth.

Thavary stiffened her fingers and struck him right in the eyeballs.

The kid reflexively reached up to protect himself, but didn't drop the screwdriver.

Thavary swept her boot under his feet. The kid went down.

She kicked away the screwdriver. Cuffed him.

Urrieta came running back.

"They must have hiding places around here." He grabbed the kid by his shirt collar and hauled him to his feet. "Well, young man, we're taking you straight to jail."

The kid ignored Urrieta. He kept his eyes on Thavary and spoke in Khmer. *"There are a lot of hungry ghosts following you."*

Thavary's breathing slowed. Sound receded, except for a rushing in her ears. Everything dimmed, except for the kid's wide, defiant face and coiled energy. His words brought something back to her. The smell of motorcycle exhaust, the dopplering effect of motorbikes passing by. A market. The shade umbrellas overhead. The shallow woven baskets. The piles of produce. Banana clusters piled high. Her grandmother's hand on her shoulder, guiding her through the crowd, stopping to gossip. The vendor had crooked teeth and said, *ghosts follow him.*

"What'd he say?" Urrieta's voice snapped her out of it.

"Kid stuff." Thavary guided the kid into the back of the patrol car and locked him in. Urrieta took the wheel so Thavary could focus on their suspect. "What's your name?"

The kid shrugged.

Thavary switched to Khmer. "*Well, here's what I know about you.*" She glanced at Urrieta, but he kept his eyes on the road. He was letting her do this her way.

"*I know that stealing cars is something kids do as part of a gang initiation.*"

The kid wrinkled his nose.

She risked another guess. "*And I know that you are trying to get initiated into the Jewel Orchid gang.*"

The boy's head swerved towards her, but he caught himself and went back to looking out the window.

"*What I can't figure out is why. You know the head of the Jewel Orchid gang was killed yesterday, right?*"

He knew. "*Doesn't matter. We got a new leader now. Younger. Better.*"

Thavary went still. This thing was bigger than she'd thought. "*Even more reason to steer clear of the gang. So why don't you tell me where you live, and we can take you home?*"

The kid remained silent.

Thavary switched to English. "Those are your choices, kid. Jail or home. You pick."

"Keo, you cuffed him." Urrieta slowed down for a red light. "We gotta take him to the precinct now. We have to book him."

Thavary kept her eyes on the kid. "Tell me where you live, or I have to let my partner take you to jail."

The kid finally spoke. "My name is Penleu."

* * *

Urrieta led the way up the walk toward the front door of the tidy ranch house. Thavary followed him, pushing Penleu ahead.

"What's that about?" Urrieta indicated the two wooden structures atop thin poles on the lawn with his chin. "Weird-looking bird houses."

"They're altars." Altars loaded with fresh fruit and large dumplings. Sticks of incense burned from small pots.

The hungry ghosts had to be fed.

Thavary rang the doorbell with her elbow, keeping a firm grip on the kid. The door was opened by a thin, middle-aged Cambodian man with hard lines around his full lips. When he saw Urrieta, he started to close the door again.

"*Pa!*"

The kid broke free from Thavary, ran to the man, and wrapped his thin arms around him. The man bent down. He was well muscled under his white shirt, just old enough that his hair was starting to thin and recede, but young enough that it was still black.

He had a muttered conversation in Khmer with the boy, too low for Thavary to hear, that ended with the boy saying, "*It's not my fault.*"

The man looked up. When his eyes met Thavary's they went wide and his mouth fell slack. He patted his son on the back. "*Go, go inside.*"

The boy took a last look at the police officers, his face flushed, and stomped off.

The man turned back to Thavary, smiling now, his back straight, his hand out to shake, American style. Thin lines snaked up from his jaw. Scars.

Urrieta shook his hand. "I'm Officer Urrieta, sir. And this is Officer Keo. You need to watch your boy more closely, sir. He was getting into trouble."

"I am very thankful that you brought him back to me,

Officers." The man answered him in English, but his eyes never left Thavary's. To her he spoke in Khmer. "*Please tell me, what kind of trouble?*"

Thavary hesitated. There seemed to be no sign of the boy's mother. Was he raising his boy alone?

Their radios crackled. When she didn't move, Urrieta said, "I'll get that. You tell him."

Thavary waited until her partner was well out of earshot. "I know this is difficult."

The man put his hand on her arm. Thavary froze.

He removed his hand, but spoke in Khmer. "*Please. Just tell me.*"

"*He was stealing a car. With a group of kids.*"

The man's gaze dropped down. His shoulders curved in toward his chest.

"*We suspect it was part of a gang initiation.*"

The man went rigid. He clenched his hands into fists.

"*I'm sorry. I know this is hard to hear.*"

When he spoke, it was in a whisper. "*It's possible that what you say is true. Ever since he lost his mother—*"

He looked at her, his eyes soft with tears, a contrast to his sharply contoured, scarred face.

She'd seen so many faces like that. Strong faces, overcome. Faces she longed to have back. Faces she didn't want to remember.

"Officer Keo." Urrieta called to her from the cruiser, the CB still in his hand.

Thavary turned toward her partner.

"*Please, we must talk.*" The man's voice was anguished. "*Please, I need your help. My boy. My boy needs your help.*"

"Just a moment, sir." She walked over to Urrieta.

"We got a noise complaint."

"Where?"

"Just a few blocks from here."

"Could you take it? I just need another minute with him."

Urrieta looked at the boy's father, still standing in the doorway. "Keo, you're a rookie. Still on probation. I'm not supposed to leave you."

"I'm a Cambo, like him." Thavary hated that term, but everyone in the department used it, so she went along with it. "Might be better if I talk to him alone."

Urrieta shrugged, his hands in the air. "Okay."

Thavary walked back to the boy's father. She heard Urrieta slam the car door shut. The tires spun in the driveway gravel.

"So, what I was trying to say, Mr.—"

"*Nam, Narith Nam. Won't you come in and have tea, and we can discuss it?*"

She stepped inside. There were shoes placed neatly on a mat by the door. The boy's shoes. His father's shoes. No women's shoes.

Thavary hesitated. She looked around at the house, listening intently, her back straight, her hand on her belt near her gun.

Furniture in the house was sparse. There were a few western-style chairs in the living room, but they were pushed against the wall. A low table centered on a large mat. A few pillows around it for seating.

"*Please, come in. I will make tea.*"

Narith waved her in, then slipped into a room off to the side. Thavary followed him.

Her tread was loud on the kitchen linoleum. Narith glanced down at her heavy police shoes, his lips in a straight line, but didn't say anything.

Thavary went back to the front door and stood on the mat. She was on duty. She couldn't remove her shoes.

Narith was still clinking around in the kitchen. She could see into the living room, where one wall was awash with color. An altar. But unlike the spirit altars outside, which were designed to placate hungry ghosts, this was a shrine to the Buddha.

Something about it made her want to get closer.

She pulled off her boots and padded into the living room

until she came face to face with the statue. A glittering silk banner served as a backdrop. Pink and white statues of the bodhisattvas circled the Buddha, bowls of camellias and miniature roses and carnations at their feet. There was a bowl of water and a plate of food.

The statue of the Buddha was a simple wood carving, much damaged and scratched but re-varnished. One hand had broken off, but had been carefully repaired.

She put her hands together and bowed her head over her fingertips. She closed her eyes. The scented candles competed with the sandalwood to perfume the room.

She followed the trail of incense to another shrine, long ago. She was little, holding on to her mother's skirt, shuffling into a temple heavy with incense and candle smoke. The statue in the shrine was the same Buddha, just bigger.

She closed her eyes tighter, trying to stay with the memory, trying to hold onto that glimpse of her mother.

"*Here is our tea.*"

Narith held out a tray with teacups and teapot, but when he saw her face his smile faded. "*Is everything all right?*"

He set the tray down on the coffee table, then handed her a paper napkin from the tray.

Thavary accepted the napkin and dried her eyes, feeling foolish. She sat down on the floor. "Let me."

Narith sat on the floor across from her. He let her pour, not speaking.

"*Mr. Nam, how old is your son?*"

"*Fourteen.*"

"*And his mother?*"

"*He has a shrine to her in his room.*"

"*She didn't make it out?*"

Narith sipped his tea. "*No. How about you? Did you lose...anyone, during that time?*"

Now it was Thavary's turn to sip her tea. Even without closing her eyes, she could see the Khmer Rouge soldiers from her hiding place, see her home aflame, hear the screams of her family within. The screams that were always with her.

She set down her cup. "*Everyone.*"

She looked back at the Buddha, the delicate crack along its wrist so carefully repaired.

"*Mr. Nam, where we came from was not a good place for children. America is definitely better. But no place is perfectly safe.*"

Narith nodded. "*You said something about a gang initiation.*"

"*Mr. Nam, your son was trying to steal a car. There were other kids with him, but he was the one trying to get the door open, the others were just watching. This behavior is typical of a gang initiation ritual.*"

Narith put down his teacup and rubbed his hands.

"*You will have to watch him very carefully. The gang wants him. They will keep after him.*"

Now it was Narith who looked over at the shrine.

"*How can I watch him? Usually I'm at the store.*" He smiled proudly. "*Hen-Heng grocery. You should come. Best Khmer grocery in Long Beach.*"

Thavary smiled. "*I'll do that.*" She took a card out of her pocket and slid it toward him. It was her foster-mother's card for the rec center. "*Take him to visit the rec center. They have many programs there, lots of fun things for kids to do after school.*"

Narith looked at the card, but didn't pick it up. "*Too many Mexicans. My boy is not so big.*"

"*It's not only Mexicans. All kinds of people go to the rec center. Mexicans, Khmer, white people—*"

"*Barangs.*" He spit out the Khmer word for foreigner as if it were a sour tasting olive.

Thavary switched to English. "This is their country. Here, we are the *barangs.*"

The doorbell rang. Thavary jumped up. "That's probably

my partner."

"Don't forget."

Thavary was already at the door, trying to force her feet back into her police boots. Narith followed her, fumbling in a pocket. Now he held something out to her.

"What's that?"

"A gift. For you." He held out a small Buddha, an exact copy of the large and battered one on his altar. "*So you remember.*" Narith Nam switched back to Khmer.

The doorbell rang again.

"Remember what?"

"We are the *barangs*. You and me."

Thavary slipped the figurine into her pocket. "Promise me you'll check out the rec center."

Narith picked up the business card. "If you promise you will come to my store." He pressed his hands together as if in prayer, held them in front of his face, and bowed slightly, the card still between his fingers.

Thavary hesitated. The *Sampeah* was a gesture of respect. As a police officer, she didn't need to do it.

But he reminded her so much of the ones she'd lost.

She sampeahed back to him.

Over the next few days, visiting the grocery store was pretty much all she thought about. But whenever she found herself nearby, she turned and went the other way.

She and Urrieta were parked in a beach parking lot, overlooking the concourse that led down to the Queen Mary.

"So, we have to plan what we're going to say at this school talk." Urrieta spooned some potato salad into his mouth.

It took Thavary a minute to answer, as her mouth was full of the *chile con queso* Urrieta's mother had packed for their lunch. "Gangs. How to spot them. How to resist."

"Those kids know more about that than we do." Urrieta

sipped his drink.

"You don't get it. The most important thing is that they see *us*. A Mexican and a Cambo, each with our own gun, and guess what, we aren't using our guns to shoot each other." Thavary grabbed up what was left of the potato salad before Urrieta could finish it.

"Hey!" Urrieta wouldn't let go.

"Calling three-boy-seven. Two-Forty-Five at a grocery on Anaheim Street. Calling three-boy-seven."

"That's us." Urrieta started the engine.

Thavary hit the flashing lights. Two-forty-five meant an assault with a deadly weapon.

Urrieta peeled out of the parking lot and headed toward Anaheim Street. He swerved up in front of the grocery and jumped out of the car, his gun drawn.

Thavary turned off the engine, put the keys in her pocket, and followed him, her gun also drawn.

The store was narrow, but numerous grocery shelves had been crammed into the small space. Green coconuts, plastic packages of dips and bottles of sauces, and packages of Tvako, a spicy sausage Thavary had longed for when she was at the refugee camp, were all over the floor.

Two Long Beach police officers Thavary recognized but had never spoken to were already in the store, one in front of the counter, one bent down behind it. The back door to the store was open, showing the way they'd come in.

"You," one of the officers called to her. "Come see if you can understand him."

Urrieta kept his gun drawn. He looked behind the door and went down each aisle.

Thavary holstered her gun and went behind the counter.

A man was half-sitting, half-lying behind the counter, two blood blooms on his torso, a baseball bat in his hands. There was blood on the bat, but Thavary was pretty sure it was his own. Had he tried to defend himself against robbers with guns with a bat?

"Sir, tell me where you are hurt."

The man looked up at her.

It was Narith Nam.

"*Penleu,*" he spoke to her in Khmer. "*My son. Go get him. They were looking for him. Don't let them find him.*"

"*I will find your son, and I will protect him. Tell me who did this to you.*"

Narith Nam approximated a shrug, then grimaced. "Gang. Mexican. Maybe. What do I know?"

His head lolled to the side. Thavary put two fingers on the side of his neck.

"Pulse is faint."

"EMTs on their way," said the police officer on the other side of the counter. "What'd he say?"

"I know him," Thavary answered. "He's worried about his son. Gangs trying to recruit the kid. He thinks that's who shot him."

"They took the money from the cash register." That was the officer behind the counter with her.

Thavary gently lifted Narith Nam's shirt. "One bullet went into his side."

She was relieved to hear the ambulance siren in the distance.

Thavary led Penleu into the busy ICU unit. Nurses consulted with residents, a doctor held court with a group of students, and fearful friends and relatives huddled around the doors to some of the rooms.

Two young Cambodians were seated in chairs on either side of Narith Nam's door. One wore a ragged cap with an emblem, the Monkey King Hanuman with his sword raised, surrounded by a gilded heraldic frame. Thavary had a brief flashback of her father in front of a television, yelling and cheering.

Soccer. King Hanuman had something to do with soccer.

The young men recognized Penleu, smiled at him and greeted him in Khmer.

Penleu tried to go into the hospital room, but Thavary stopped him.

"Let me go in first. Then I'll come get you."

Penleu gave her that wide-eyed frowning look she was getting to know very well. The soccer fan smiled at Penleu, took off his soccer cap, and put it on Penleu's head, pulling it over his eyes. Penleu snatched the cap off and put it back on the man, now covering his eyes. Clearly a game they'd played before.

Thavary went into Narith Nam's room.

The door was slightly ajar, but the room was dimly lit. The noise from the hallway didn't block out the regular beep-beep-beeping of the heart monitor.

Thavary approached Narith Nam's bedside. She counted the number of tubes.

Narith's eyes fluttered open. He looked dazed, but he spoke to her in English. "Officer Keo. I am very happy to see you again."

"Sorry it has to be like this." She glanced at the nurse's instructions on the dryboard.

Narith lifted his right hand and indicated his side. "Bullet went through my ribs. Made my lung collapse. Now I have a tube. It will let the air out. Then I can go home."

Thavary sat in the chair next to the bed. "That's really good to hear. What about your leg?"

Narith grimaced. "That will take a bit longer."

He looked down at the shape of his legs under the blanket, then back at her. "How is my boy?"

"He's right outside. I'll bring him in. But I need to ask you something first, Mr. Nam."

"Call me Narith."

"Who are the two men guarding your door?"

"They work for me, at the store."

"If you're worried about your safety, I can ask my sergeant to assign you a police guard."

"It's not necessary."

Thavary felt a quiver of doubt in her stomach. "Do you remember what you said to me, in your store? You said gang members shot you. The gang that wants your son."

Narith shook his head. "I was robbed. Not by gang. Crazy guys. Don't know how to use a gun. Luckily for me." The smile flickered over his face again. For a moment he looked younger, handsomer, vulnerable.

Thavary felt a wave of warmth spread from her chest to her feet and her fingers. The feeling was strange to her, alien. She shifted her feet around, trying to restore her sense of balance.

Narith stirred again. "But my son—I have no relatives here—can you watch him?"

"I can do that. Now let me bring him in, he's very worried about you."

Narith smiled, his face softer in the dim hospital light than Thavary had ever seen it before. "Yes, my boy, my boy."

Penleu lost his cool when Urrieta pulled up in front of the rec center. He yanked his arm out of Thavary's grasp. "I can't go in there."

He strode a few feet away from her with an *I-don't-know-her* turn to his shoulder.

Only to scurry back when a group of Chicanos came out of the rec center, shoving each other and laughing.

Their laughter froze when they saw Penleu, then resumed, forced this time, when they saw Thavary and Urrieta in their police uniforms.

Thavary put her hand on his shoulder. "I'll introduce you to a couple people. Then you'll be fine."

He swatted her hand off, but went along.

Thavary led him over to Melanie, her foster mother. "This

is Moms. And I'll tell you a secret. There are snacks in that desk drawer."

"Penleu! How nice to see you! And, Thavary! Don't give away all my secrets!" Melanie pulled the drawer open and pulled out two bags. "What'll it be, chips, or cookies?"

Penleu took both.

Thavary looked at the kids doing homework. Kids playing games. Kids just hanging out. Penleu was right: most of them were Chicano or Mexican. She would ask her boss to increase the patrol around the rec center. If the grocery store really was a gang hit, a Khmer gang might decide to hit the rec center in retaliation.

In just a few days Narith Nam was back on his feet. He insisted on re-opening the store. "My employees need to work," he told Thavary. "And people need to know we're open."

Thavary and Urrieta organized the security. Local news covered the event. There was much posturing by various dignitaries about brave businessmen like Narith Nam. The fact that the Hen-Heng grocery was re-opening was a sign that the gang wars wouldn't define the neighborhood.

The same men that had guarded Narith's door at the hospital, one still wearing his beat-up cap with the monkey-king soccer emblem, held the ribbon while Penleu cut it.

Narith Nam stood straight and tall and refused to use his cane as long as the cameras rolled. Even injured, he radiated confidence, as he and Penleu beamed for the news cameras.

He seems taller. More powerful. Even after taking three bullets.

Narith Nam was not just any grocer. He was a man with a history. She wondered what it was. Who had he been? What had he lost?

After the news trucks left, Narith offered the officers cold sodas. Urrieta nodded. Narith turned and went back into the store, and Thavary followed him.

Narith reached into a cooler and pulled out a bottle of Jarritos soda.

"*How are you feeling?*" Thavary switched to Khmer.

"*Glad to be back.*" Then he admitted, "*Getting tired.*" He handed her the bottle, but when she took it, he didn't let go right away. "*It would be a great honor if you could come to my house tomorrow. I will make you good Khmai dinner. To thank you for all your help.*"

Thavary hesitated.

"*Penleu would also be very pleased.*"

Thavary bowed her head and agreed.

When Narith let her in he accepted her box of cakes. His eyes traveled over her straight black hair, now hanging loose, and the dress. "*I have never seen you without your uniform. Very nice.*"

In the kitchen, Penleu was hunched over the stove. Thavary watched Narith guide his son through the steps of sautéing the marinated beef for the *lok lak*. She was struck again by Narith Nam's toned and powerful body.

Maybe he's not that old. Maybe it's just the war on his face.

Penleu was losing his temper. "*Why can't she cook it?*"

Thavary shook her head. "*I can make hamburgers. I don't know how to cook Khmai.*"

"*Then I have to teach both of you.*" Narith waved her over.

Penleu ducked out from under his father's arm and escaped. Thavary turned after him but Narith said, "*Let him go, let him go. Now you learn.*"

Thavary tried to follow his directions, but the aroma of garlic and fish sauce, soy and lime, sent her back to her mother's kitchen. She closed her eyes and waited, hoping her memory would send her a glimpse of her mother over the stove back in Cambodia, or maybe of her father at the table.

28

"*You're letting it burn.*" Narith took over the cooking, turning the strips of beef, scooping them into a bowl.

"*My mother used to make this.*"

He set the bowl of meat on a tray. "*Ah. I thought you were too young to remember.*"

Thavary's heart, usually cold and small, felt full and big. Her throat felt thick, so her voice came out low. "*You help me. You help me remember.*"

Narith's smile wiped all the hardness off his sharp features.

When Penleu went to bed, Thavary got up to leave. She thought Narith might try to keep her there longer, but wasn't sure if she was ready for that.

But when he didn't try to keep her there, the same part of her that had been ready to rush out now moved slowly. *He's still part of an active case. Better to keep a distance.*

Narith followed her to the door and watched as she slipped her feet back into her flats.

"*I would like to meet your barangs.*" He pointed at the ceiling. "*Thank them too. For watching my boy.*"

Thavary nodded. "*Melanie, my foster mother, would like that.*"

"*I would like to ask her also for her permission.*"

"*For what?*" Thavary reached down to pull on the stiff new shoe.

"*To court you.*"

The part of her that had wanted to leave, then wanted to stay, now stood frozen. One side of her was flattered. One side of her was offended.

That side won. She straightened up. "In America, the only permission you need is mine."

Some emotion crossed his eyes. Was he offended by her straightforwardness? Or hurt by her tone?

She leaned toward him and planted a kiss on his lips, warm,

wet, and soft. But not lingering.

Without waiting for his reaction, she went out the door.

Thavary always stopped at the rec center after she and Urrieta finished their rounds. Melanie was always quick to say Penleu hadn't come in, not since his father had gotten out of the hospital.

"Probably helping out at home." But inwardly Thavary feared she'd been too forward. Narith Nam was clearly very traditional. Perhaps he'd misunderstood the way she'd kissed him.

So when she stopped at the rec center days later and found Penleu taking his pick out of Melanie's snack drawer, her heart jumped.

"We've been talking about you for hours," Melanie said. "He wants to know everything about you."

A burst of yelling from the game room. Melanie hurried off.

Thavary reached into Penleu's chip bag.

"My dad is coming to get me. He said to tell you he wants to see you."

Thavary followed him outside. Sure enough, there was Narith Nam, just parking his car. As soon as he saw her, there was that smile again.

"Can we walk?"

They walked to the beach, not speaking, Penleu running ahead of them.

I made the first move. Now it's his turn.

Narith picked a camellia, reached up to put it in her hair, but was blocked by her cap. "I'm going to open another store," he said. "More than one, eventually. Plenty of Cambodians here."

Thavary took the flower from him. "That's good. You can hire boys like your son. Keep them out of the gangs."

Her eyes went to Penleu, now kicking up sand by the water's edge. "Melanie, my foster mother, wants to see your store.

She wants to learn how to make *lok lak*."

"I will be happy to show her." Narith turned toward her, waiting.

Thavary looked at the flower in her hand, the white petals already browning at the edges, their softness such a contrast to her uniform.

"I just joined the force, you know. I like being a cop. We need Khmer cops."

Narith watched Penleu too, who was now playing chicken with the incoming surf, running towards it and jumping back.

"Also, I'm only ten years older than he is. Not even old enough to be his mother."

Narith turned to her. He took her hand. "You and me, we live in two worlds. The world that we left, which we still carry, here—" he gestured to his heart, "—and this new world, the *barang* world." He glanced at his son just as Penleu miss-timed the incoming surf and found water rushing over his feet. He looked back at them, the chagrin clearly etched on his face. Narith waved at him and smiled. "He doesn't remember the old country. He only knows this world. I try to make him remember, but it's not working."

He turned back to Thavary. "It's very lonely, to have lost it all. It helps to remember with someone."

Thavary thought of the screaming at night in the refugee camp, the way she and other young girls had to hide from the roving gangs. "Not all the memories are good."

Narith squeezed her hand. "In one way, this world is like the old world. To survive, you have to fight. You and I, we know this. You and I, we're fighters. We are the same. I recognize that in you. You recognize that in me. That's important. That's what matters."

He stepped closer, pulled off her hat. Thavary thought he might kiss her, but he took the flower from her hand and placed it in her hair. "Remember, you can't be a police officer all the time. Sometimes—" he stroked her hair, "—sometimes we just have to be like this, a man, a woman."

Then he kissed her, not like the *barangs* she'd kissed in high school who tilted their heads to the side, but nose to nose.

Penleu hollered. A wave crashed over him. He jumped up and down in the water, screaming with joy.

There was a banging on the door. It worked its way into Thavary's regular nightmare about the fire, her family screaming and pounding on the doors.

"Thavary! Thavary! Wake up!"

It was Urrieta's voice. Thavary jumped out of bed. She saw her utility belt, her gun. She wasn't in Cambodia anymore. She was in Long Beach, California. She was safe. And she had a job to do.

Urrieta was outside, geared up, the light on the cruiser flashing. "Finally. You sure can sleep. Come on, we gotta go, there's a fire, they need us to do crowd control."

"Why didn't you call me?"

"I did. Multiple times."

Why didn't Moms wake me?

Her mother's car wasn't in the driveway.

Thavary got into the cruiser. "Where's the fire?"

"It's the rec center."

Thavary's heartbeat slowed. *Moms.*

"Come on, Urrieta, step on it."

After what she'd been through during the war in Cambodia, after what she'd experienced in the refugee camp, Thavary thought she could keep her cool during any emergency. But now her feet felt like blocks of ice, and her hands were clumsy.

"Good thing it's after hours," Urrieta said as they took in the fire fighters trying to douse the flames in one corner of the building.

Then Thavary saw it. Her moms' old gas-guzzler parked in

its usual spot by the rec center. She pointed at her mother's car. "Moms," she squeaked.

She dove out of the car and ran through the crowd, looking into the faces of the bystanders. She looked at the ambulance. The back doors were open, but no one was getting treated. She was only dimly aware of Urrieta's voice behind her telling her to wait and something about smoke.

She knew exactly where her mother would be. In her office, working on a grant application. The center always needed more funds, was always going broke.

Thavary ran around to the side of the building not red with fire. The door was locked, but Thavary had her own key.

Inside, the building was pitch dark and full of smoke. Thavary lit her flashlight and made her way, more by memory than sight, to Moms' office. The smoke burned her eyes, her throat, left an acrid taste on her tongue, so dense she couldn't see anything, even with the flashlight.

Her eyes burned. Her throat already raw as if scraped with something sharp.

The door to her mother's office was shut. Thavary tried to open it but couldn't.

She kicked and kicked at the door hinges, but the door would not give.

Then she felt a hand on her shoulder and whirled around. Two firefighters behind her, wearing masks. They held a mask out to her. Thavary ignored it and instead wrestled the axe out of the second firefighter's hands and went back to hacking at the door.

The firefighters pushed her out of the way, dropped the mask next to her, and took over. *Thud! Crack! Bang!*

Thavary bent down to retrieve the gas mask. As she lifted it up she saw something else on the floor.

An old, battered cap. With a soccer team logo on it.

Hanuman the monkey king, his sword raised, set in a gilded heraldic frame.

The cap meant something important, but her thoughts were scrambled, she couldn't remember what. She reached for it.

Crash! The firefighters had broken down the door. More smoke roiled in.

Too Dark. Can't breathe.

She tried to pull the gas mask on. She'd taken a class on how to use it, but now she couldn't remember how it worked.

The firemen dragged someone past her. Thavary tried to reach up to them, but couldn't move her hand.

"Moms," Thavary cried. But no sound came out.

Another masked face loomed over her, reached down, and lifted her up. Not a firefighter. A police officer.

The cap. I have to get the cap.

She passed out.

Thavary sat in an unmarked car across the street from Narith Nam's house. The altars were filled with fresh food. The sprinklers swished, the lawn sparkled. She watched Narith walk out with Penleu and accompany him to the corner, standing there until the school bus arrived and Penleu got on it.

She got out of the car. They'd given her a couple days off, so she wore jeans, a T-shirt, a leather jacket.

Narith Nam's face lit up. "*Thavary, how wonderful to see you. Please, please come in.*"

Thavary answered him in English. "I only have a moment."

"I saw the news," Narith switched to English. "You are a hero. You saved your *barang*-mother."

"Not me. The firefighters. Yes, she was lucky. But the rec center is very damaged. It will be shut down for months. Maybe even permanently."

"Do they know what caused the fire?"

Thavary thought of Penleu, screaming joyously in the surf. Of the way Narith had kissed her. The healing he'd offered.

"Arson. Almost killed my moms." In spite of her resolve,

her voice cracked.

"Please, Thavary, come in, have tea." There it was, that soft look in his eyes she'd fallen in love with.

Thavary didn't move. Tears streamed down her cheeks.

"Thavary." He wrapped his arms around her, held her to him. "Shhh. Shhh. Everything is okay. I'm here."

Thavary put her arms around him, rested her head on his chest for a moment. She couldn't feel a holster, but a man like Narith Nam wouldn't necessarily need a weapon. She ducked out of his embrace. "I know who you really are." She watched his face carefully, some part of her still hoping she was wrong. "I know you are the new head of the Jewel Orchid gang. Your men started the fire."

Narith's face went completely still, the smile gone, as if it had never been.

Thavary watched his smile fade. Her skin tightened, as if something were crawling on her, so tight her ribs felt squeezed. Her face and ears went hot, remembering how she'd kissed those lips.

Narith looked around. Checking to see if she was alone. "You don't have proof, or you wouldn't be here."

"The proof burnt up in the fire. But I know it, and that's enough."

"Thavary." He reached for her.

Thavary's hand moved to her holster. "Touch me and I will use this."

"I see." Narith lowered his hands, but didn't step back. "So, you think you know me."

"I thought I knew you. But you were just using me. You needed someone on the inside."

Now his expression did change. The soft look in his eyes, a look she had only seen on his face when he looked at Penleu and at her, returned. "That was my plan, at first. I heard about this new cop, the first Khmai cop on the force. I thought it would be easy."

He stopped and looked around, then looked back at her. "But then I saw you. You are so beautiful. I felt—" he put his hand on his chest. "We are the same, Thavary. You and I. We know what the world is really like. We're both warriors. We understand each other. That's rare."

"You're initiating your own son. I don't understand that."

"That's because you grew up with *barangs*. This is our world. Come with me, Thavary. Join us. Open your heart to me, the way I opened mine to you."

"Disband the gang."

If she'd had any hope, any hope at all, it dissipated entirely when she saw his face return to its stony look.

"Too late for that now. I would be a dead man. Penleu too."

For a moment, the only sound was the swish-swish-swish of the sprinklers. Narith kept his eyes on her face, studying her, as if he were trying to memorize every detail.

"Penleu." Thavary said.

"What?"

"If you really love him, keep *him* out of the gang."

Now Narith did step back. "He's my only son. I did all this for him."

Thavary stepped forward. "This is what I'll do for him. I'm going to bring you down. I'm going to bring you down and I'm going to get Penleu away from you and he'll be raised by *barangs*. Like me."

"You were raised by *barangs*. But you're Khmer. Don't forget."

Thavary took a last look at the face she'd thought would save her from her demons. "Yes. I'm Khmer. I'm American. And I'm a cop."

She turned away from him and walked back to her car.

COINCIDENCE
Mark Hague

Those few seconds are seared on my eyeballs, in my memory. The lone white kid hitting the black one. At the last minute, pushing him off the platform right onto the rails. My reflexes were automatic, I even pressed my left foot down on the non-existent brake pedal and cranked the hand brake until I thought it would break off. But a train is tons of steel and they don't stop on a dime.

Was there any way I could have stopped the train in time? Coming into the 103rd Street/Watts Towers station, I'd done everything by the book, had even been going slower than normal. Especially after seeing the skirmish on the platform.

I was there for hours. It was all a blur, calling the dispatcher and watching as another train arrived to take passengers on to their destination. What wasn't a blur was the fight and the boy sailing off the edge of the platform. I can still see the body bag on the gurney where they'd stowed the pieces. I went over it again and again with the police detective, described the scuffle, the pushing. I could even describe the killer down to the type of sneakers he was wearing as he nonchalantly walked down away the ramp with no one trying to stop him. I could even describe his jazzy orange sneakers (the latest style I think) and the red T-shirt he wore, with its band logo, The Fetid Swamp.

I asked for a leave of absence, drank my way through the following weekend, the following week, trying to forget what I'd seen, trying to stop the play-by-play before my eyes for days, weeks, months afterwards.

I sought out a therapist. "How did that make you feel?" he asked. How the hell was it supposed to make me feel? My train ran over a kid, severed his head, his legs. How do you deal with that? How do you go back to living normally, like it had never happened? How do you forget?

My description was accurate—I can still see every excruciating detail, every movement, every jab and punch and push in those last seconds before the kid's body went over the edge. The assailant—I was later able to learn his name—Peter Miller, what a perfectly ordinary name—and the victim's—Keanu Jacobs. I sat through the trial—I was a witness in the Compton Courthouse. And I pointed at Peter Miller when asked to identify the assailant—just as I had at the Compton Police Department when given the books of photos to look through. Did I solemnly swear to tell the truth, the whole truth, and nothing but the truth? Yeah, fuck yeah, I did. But the Miller kid's father had hired a damned good attorney. "Is there any doubt that you saw what you think you saw?" No, no there wasn't. I knew what I saw. But his lawyer pointed out that my eyesight had changed since my last prescription and since I hadn't been back to an optometrist, perhaps I hadn't seen what I thought I saw. Bullshit. I could see perfectly well thank you, and I swore on the stand to tell the truth. I remember the kid smirking at me while I sat in the witness stand, trying to figure out how to answer the prosecutor and the attorney. And I saw the kid point his two fingers from his eyes to me with a glare of hatred and rage.

"So, you can't be sure that you actually saw the defendant on the platform, right?" his lawyer asked me, after establishing that I hadn't gotten new eyeglasses yet. He smiled at the jury and quirked his eyebrow. They smiled.

"Yes, I know what I saw. I saw the defendant push the other kid onto the tracks. It was clear as day!" I shouted. The damned lawyer was making me look like a fool about the glasses thing. Even if my eyesight had changed, I could see well enough.

"Just answer the question," the judge admonished. I tried to calm down, but the lawyer had me rattled. He was good, I have to give him that.

The kid walked. Any other witnesses had scattered. I was the only one who had come forward to tell what I'd seen. It wasn't good enough. He walked.

"It's not your fault," my therapist told me over and over. And, yeah, intellectually, I knew it wasn't. I hadn't been in that fight, hadn't pushed the Jacobs kid off the platform, and there was no way I could have stopped the train. But try telling yourself that at three in the fucking morning, lying there sweating and remembering seeing the kid fall off the platform and try to forget the sound of bones splintering, crushed by tons of steel. Okay, okay, I probably didn't actually hear it over the squeal of the brakes, but that became part of my memory, even so.

After the trial, the phone calls started. I'd answer and there was only silence. Once I heard the whisper, "I'll get you." And that was the message scrawled on the front of my apartment in red paint. I moved and changed my phone number twice.

I couldn't go back to work for months. He'd fall off the platform fifty times a night and I would cry out, sobbing uncontrollably. Yes, I knew it wasn't my fault, knew that I couldn't have stopped the train. But what if—what if I could have? Could I have reacted sooner? If only I hadn't been working overtime because someone had called in sick. No, no, I knew it wasn't my fault. Knew I'd done everything I could have. But there was still that niggling doubt, that wondering in the corner of my mind at three o'clock in the fucking morning.

The doubt grew in the dark recesses. I even thought of killing myself. I wanted an end to reliving that scene day in and day out. And knew that no matter how long I lived I'd never forget what had happened, see that kid falling. Over and over, again and again.

But I didn't kill myself. Obviously. Yeah, okay, I should have quit, gotten another job. I didn't quit, but I did go out on interviews for other jobs, as a guard, a security officer, clerking in a 7-Eleven. When my medical leave ran out, I went back, but I found myself surveilling each platform at each station more carefully, and jumping at any untoward movement, ready to apply the brakes, breaking out into a cold sweat, even when everything was calm, normal.

By three months later, I was finally able to relax. I'd only encountered minor and routine problems, and no longer jumped at sudden movements. No longer broke out in icy perspiration when pulling into a station. Yes, whenever I closed my eyes I saw that scene play out, but it began to fade a little. I tried to forget; alcohol and meds didn't help much. That little fucker's face still smirked in my mind and the poor kid who died, I still saw his severed head when I'd run out of the cab to see if he could still be alive, knowing that was impossible.

I'd never drunk so much before, maybe a few beers sometimes, but now I was drinking every damned night, trying to blot out the memory, trying to forget. I knew I was drinking too much. I was afraid that I'd relive those moments forever. I never allowed the alcohol to affect my work, though, always made sure that I was completely sober when I went to work. I knew I needed to be alert, at least when I was in the cab.

Then, nearly a year later, I was back on that old schedule and I was doing all right. I mean, yeah, I couldn't forget, not entirely, but I was trying. One afternoon I was pulling into Firestone Station contemplating being off after two more runs, being able to go home, to another nightmare-wracked night. I was looking ahead obsessively, like always, and saw it again.

On the platform, an arm swung forward, a punch landed. There were several people fighting now. Pushing and punching. Black, white. I automatically pushed on the hand lever to slow the train, even though it wasn't time yet and we hadn't come close enough to the station. I felt the train jerk behind me then slow down incrementally. Hoping no one had been injured, thrown off-balance, I pushed harder on the hand brake.

And just like before, a body catapulted off the platform and lay on the tracks.

This kid was lying there just as Jacobs had, looking up. I couldn't believe it. Orange shoes, red T-shirt. The same band. It couldn't be Peter Miller, could it? I blinked. Again. It was him. He was even dressed the same as in my memory. At least this time I could stop the train in time. I—I wasn't a judge, a jury, an executioner. I was only a train engineer.

I *could* still stop in time...

DARKNESS
KEEPS CHASING
Peter Sexton

Laswell heard the distant hiss of rubber gliding over slick pavement as a lone car passed overhead along the Olympic Boulevard bridge in the wet darkness of the rainy, winter night. The instructions had been clear: come alone or the girl dies.

At 3 a.m., there wasn't much traffic on the streets above nor another soul to be found down here in the belly of the Los Angeles River. Ditching his back-up hadn't been difficult, though there would no doubt be hell to pay tomorrow.

So be it.

This was his daughter.

Fuck procedure!

Detective Bill Laswell scanned the area carefully but found no vehicles or subdued sources of light, nothing to indicate potential danger. Directly beneath the bridge, about a hundred yards in front of him, he saw the silhouette of a girl strapped to a large wooden pallet leaning against the concrete support pillar. From this distance, through the rain and darkness, Laswell couldn't be certain if was indeed his daughter, Laurie.

Once again, he scanned the area.

Darkness.

Silence.

Laswell drew his Glock .9mm from the holster on his hip, held it alongside his right leg. He began moving toward the dark image under the bridge.

The rain gave no sign of showing mercy, and Laswell already carried additional weight from the dampness of his coat.

Another car crossed on the bridge above.

Laswell scanned the area again.

Nothing.

He crept toward the dark shape.

Seventy yards...sixty yards...fifty...

He recognized the girl. Her short, blonde hair. The striped front-tie blouse...a gift from him on her thirteenth birthday.

Laurie.

He picked up his pace, fighting the urge to run.

Calm, level head. *Don't fuck this up.*

Twenty-five yards now.

He saw the fear in her eyes...the tears, the bruising, the swelling across the left side of her face.

One last glance around...

Still alone.

"It's all right, honey," Laswell said, keeping his voice low. "I'm here now. You're safe."

Tears streamed down the girl's face. Blood crusted beneath her nose and her upper-lip. Fear on his daughter's face burned a hole deep into his heart. Yes—he would kill the bastard who'd done this to his little girl. *Absolutely.* When Laswell tracked him down, there would be no badge, there would be no oath to protect and to serve. There would only be justice. Delivered swiftly. With severe purpose and intent.

Laurie shook her head, fought against the ties that bound her.

Laswell holstered his weapon and reached for the gag in his daughter's mouth.

She shook her head as vigorously as the binds would allow.

Laswell carefully pulled the dirty white cloth from the girl's mouth.

"Daddy!" Laurie cried at once. "I'm so sorry. I—!"

A sudden explosion of gunfire boomed over her voice.

Laswell struggled with the girl's restraints, feverishly tugging at the unyielding plastic zip ties.

More gunfire.

But from where?

The rainfall and the echo down here in the concrete river made pinpointing the location of the shooter next to impossible.

Laswell pulled his knife from his pocket and cut Laurie free of her restraints.

She crumpled to the concrete, no doubt her legs exhausted from being forced to stand for who knows how long.

"Come on, honey." Laswell lifted her from the ground and carried her behind the support pillar.

More shots pierced through the dark night.

Though it seemed as though several minutes had passed, Laswell knew it couldn't have been more than just a few seconds.

Now, crouched behind the pillar with his daughter, Detective Bill Laswell returned fire.

Three weeks later...

Bill Laswell stood at the edge of the grass, hesitant, solemn, staring at the bouquet of irises and orchids in his right hand. This early in the morning, Rose Hills Memorial Park was quiet, peaceful...More private.

He tore his eyes away from the flowers he clutched and looked across the lush green park. He took one last drag of his cigarette, dropped it to the asphalt and smashed it beneath his shoe. This short walk had already begun to fill him with anger and self-loathing. Still, he would take this walk no less than twice a week for the rest of his days on Earth.

He forced himself to look down at the memorial plaque. Tears filled his eyes as he read those words again.

In Loving Memory, Beloved Daughter, Laurie Laswell, June 5, 2004—April 17, 2018.

He no longer heard his girl's screams from that night. Not long ago replaced by those soft, sad words.

I'm sorry, Daddy.

He heard her voice every night. Couldn't blot out that voice even if he wanted to. And every night, he answered. "No, honey. *I'm* sorry. I failed you."

His eyes widened as he glanced at the flowers in his hand, as though he were seeing them for the first time. "I brought your favorite flowers." He stooped and placed the bouquet into the flower cup alongside the plaque. He wondered what had happened to the flowers he'd brought on his last visit.

"Honey." Voice lowered, he looked around to make sure he was alone. "I'm going to find the man who did this." He paused, then added. "I swear to you, I will."

Laswell rose to his feet. He was about to turn and leave when he remembered something else he wanted to tell his daughter.

"I smoked my last cigarette today. I know I've been promising you I'd quit." More tears welled in his eyes. "I'm sorry I didn't do it while you were still here to see."

Laswell rested at his desk at police headquarters on West 1st Street. A growing stack of case files sat next to his computer keyboard. He laid his hand on the stack, let it rest there for a few moments before he dragged his fingers over the manila folders. He lifted the first one from the pile. Glanced at the label. Tossed it back onto the stack. He couldn't focus on other cases right now.

He lifted a framed photograph from his desk. Stared at it... He remembered this moment as if it were just yesterday. He and his wife, Kate, had taken Laurie to the Griffith Observatory for her tenth birthday. It was all she had talked about for months afterward.

When he glanced around the squad room, he saw that the other detectives avoided making eye-contact. He understood their need to do this. What happened to him and his family was a reminder that anyone who wore a badge was a target— and that the people they loved were *also* at risk.

Laswell opened his side drawer and removed the blue murder book he knew he would find there. Did he want to do this? Did he want to open the book? Look at the crime scene photos? See his daughter like that?

No. He...

What the hell?

The corner of a PostIt note peeked from between the murder book's pages.

He opened the book to the note. His partner's cramped writing.

Patrick Walsh aka Lizard. Inez Street, Boyle Heights. Print lifted from Laurie's cell phone.

Laswell plucked his cell phone from his belt and called his partner's number.

Voicemail.

"Hey, partner. Just saw the note about Patrick Walsh. I need to talk to the guy myself. Heading to his home now. If you get this in time, feel free to meet me there."

There was only one explanation as to how Walsh's fingerprint ended up on Laurie's phone: he was the asshole who had made the call that night. His was the voice on the other end of the phone telling Laswell where to go if he wanted to save his daughter. Walsh may not have actually *killed* her, but he would know who did. One way or the other, he was going to spill his guts.

Why hadn't his partner called him as soon as he received the results from the lab? Why hadn't he called as soon as he had learned they had not only found a print but matched it to someone in the system?

The house on Inez Street looked quiet. Laswell called his partner's number again.

Straight to voicemail.

He contemplated calling for back-up but decided he would feel out the situation first, figure out what he had.

On the porch, he stood to one side, drew his Glock, then knocked on the screen door.

"LAPD," he shouted.

No answer.

He knocked harder.

"LAPD," he shouted again.

No response.

He pulled the screen open and tried the doorknob.

The door creaked open on old, tired hinges.

He followed the Glock inside just two steps, cleared the room, then called out again.

No answer.

He continued into the house as he searched for Patrick Walsh, aka Lizard.

The stench of spoiled food bled from the kitchen and assaulted his nose. Smelled like no one had been here for several days.

Search completed. No sign of Walsh.

Must have skipped town. Hiding, and waiting until the heat died down before he would resurface.

Back at his desk, Laswell combed through the jacket they had on Patrick Walsh. A few misdemeanors, a couple of felonies, nothing that jumped off the page and screamed *Hey, I'm the shooter. I did your daughter.* Many of the charges leveled against him had been dismissed. In all, Lizard did time for only one of the felonies...and not much time at that. His experience told Laswell that Lizard was being used as a CI. That's the only explanation for so many brushes with the law and so little jail time.

If he could identify his handler within the department, maybe he could learn where he might be found.

Only the chief had access to handler information. For now, Laswell would try and work around this. If something didn't break for him soon, he would visit the chief and call in a marker. The chief owed him a favor. It might just be time to collect.

For now, Detective Laswell pulled the files on all cases where Lizard had been charged. Maybe he could find a common thread, notice a name that kept popping up...*something.*

It was grunt work, the sort of thing assigned to a D1, rather than a veteran detective. But Laswell was off the books on this one, not officially assigned to the case. And besides, he couldn't trust anyone else to see what he would see, or to reach the same conclusions, make the same connections. So, he made himself comfortable and began reviewing the files one by one.

It was close to midnight when Laswell found his wife in the kitchen. Doing dishes this late at night?

Oh, Kate.

He stood back and watched her. She was crying, and that made him feel even worse about the lateness of his arrival. He walked up behind her. "I'm sorry, Kate. I completely lost track of time."

She didn't answer, didn't turn to face him, though she paused in her task for a moment to gaze out the window. Then: "I was at the cemetery today." She began to sob.

Laswell reached to take her into his arms but hesitated

when she spoke.

"I wish I could be mad at you," she said. "I *want* to be mad at you. Maybe that would make this all a little easier." She took a breath, wiped tears from her eyes with the back of her wrist. "Maybe nothing can do that for me now."

"Oh, Kate. I know." He took a step closer. "I've been running myself ragged trying to figure out what happened that night." He waited for her to respond. When she didn't, he said, "I didn't see the whole picture. Knowing it was our daughter...knowing it was Laurie...it made me careless."

"You promised me you would never let anything happen to her." Kate's sobbing grew stronger. "You *promised!*"

Laswell didn't know what else to say. Every response he thought of..."I'm going to find the bastard who did this," he finally said, though the words seemed to fall flat.

Kate turned from the sink then, stared at him for a long moment. "I'm trying not to hate you."

Nine hours before the call...

Recognizing his wife's ringtone, Laswell spoke as soon as he answered. "I know, I know, I'm running late again. I'm on the road now—"

"Bill, Laurie's missing." Kate sounded frightened.

"What? What do you mean she's missing?"

"She didn't come home from school. At first I thought she had just stopped off somewhere with friends...but then I got worried and started making some calls."

"I'm sure she's fine," Bill said. "Probably with that boy she's been talking about lately."

"No, Bill, she's *gone!* I found a note."

"*What?*"

"I didn't see it at first because it was in her coat pocket. The coat she hasn't taken off since you brought it home for her birthday." A sob. "The coat was on her bed."

Laswell hit the lights and siren on his detective sedan and accelerated through the city streets.

"I'll be home in five minutes," he told his wife. "Where's the note now?"

"When I saw what it was, I set it down on the bed. I haven't touched it since."

Good, Laswell thought. *Maybe we'll get lucky.* God, *let us get lucky.*

Within four hours, the Laswell residence was swarming with uniform cops, detectives, and crime scene technicians. Lieutenant Lisa Lewis pulled Laswell aside, away from the others and to the quiet of the guest bedroom.

"How you holding up?" Lewis asked. She leaned her tall, fit frame back against the door they had just come through.

"Under the circumstances…"

"I know," she told him, "this whole thing is shit." She held his eyes, then added, "Anything you need, just say the word."

"Thanks, L-T. I'm good."

Another long moment.

"No, you're not," she told him.

She was right—he wasn't.

"We'll find her." Lewis placed her hand on his shoulder and stared into his eyes. "Everything's going to work out fine."

"Yeah," he said.

He wanted to believe her.

The next two hours passed in a restless blur. With no idea where to begin looking for Laurie, all anyone could do was sit by the phones and hope for the best. Laswell watched Lt. Lisa Lewis talking with his wife, soothing her, calming her. He was glad she was here. It allowed him to focus on finding his daughter.

James Gray, the best print man they had in the department, was dusting every square inch of Laurie's bedroom, every surface her abductor might possibly have touched. The chance was better than good that the perp had worn some kind of gloves, but they had to try anyway.

Laswell said, "Tell me something good, Jim. I'm going out of my fucking mind here."

The forensic print tech shook his head. "Nothing, Laz. Not a damn thing. Looks like our guy wore gloves."

Laswell's cell phone rang. He sprinted to the kitchen table and to his phone, now alongside Kate's and the house phone. The tech boys had them all ready to track any incoming call, pinpoint the caller's location in a matter of seconds. Laswell waited for the go-ahead.

Finally, he grabbed the phone, then said, "Laswell."

No response.

"Who is this?"

Dial tone.

Whoever it was...gone.

Laswell glanced at his wife. The look on her face hurt him worse than being slammed in the gut with a battering ram. It was the fear; it was the pain. But, most of all, it was the loss of hope. He was about to go to her, but the phone rang again.

He consulted his watch: 2:32 a.m.

A male voice was on the other end of the line. The call disconnected after just forty-three seconds.

"This is my daughter," Laswell shouted.

"Exactly," Lewis said, "which is why you need to listen to what I'm telling you. You're not thinking like a cop—you're thinking like a father. You can't trust your own judgment right now."

Laswell shook his head. "No...this has to be done *my* way. I can't take any chances."

Fresh tears in her eyes, Kate pushed past the cluster of law enforcement personnel surrounding her husband. "Bill... *please,*" she pleaded. "You can't do this alone. Let them help. You have the support of the entire department. Use it."

Time was his enemy. The longer it took him to get to his

daughter the worse her chances of survival.

"Fine," he said. "How do we do this? They're expecting me to come alone."

"We'll put someone in the backseat of your car," Lewis said. "We'll track your cell so we know where they send you."

Laswell's partner, Steven Jacoby, said, "I'll go, L-T."

Lewis nodded. "Body armor, both of you. We're not taking any chances."

"Fine," Laswell said, "let's do this. We're wasting time."

"I'm gonna get the vest from my trunk," Jacoby said. "I'll meet you at your car."

Laswell waited by the side of the house, watching Jacoby wait for him beside his black Crown Vic. After about three minutes, Jacoby set the vest on the hood and went back into the house, presumably to find out what was taking so long. As soon as Jacoby was gone, Laswell hustled out to his car, tossed Jacoby's vest to the ground, along with his own cell phone, then climbed into the car and sped away before his partner returned.

Three days after Laurie's shooting...

Patrick Walsh opened the blinds and let some light into his bedroom. He removed pants and shirts from his dresser drawers and sat them beside his socks and underwear. From the same drawer, he removed a .22 caliber Beretta Bobcat, grabbed the loaded seven-round magazine, and slid it into the gun. Then he pushed the compact pistol into his pants pocket. He retrieved a small suitcase from his closet and opened it. He hurried around the room, grabbing everything that mattered to him: photos, letters, important papers. He set all of it on the bed, then moved to the bathroom.

He opened the medicine cabinet, removed a can of shaving cream, twisted the top off and poured the contents onto the counter. A secret hiding place for valuables, the can held all the money he had to his name. Walsh didn't need to count the dirty bills from the can; he knew exactly how much money was there. It wasn't a lot, but it would have to do.

Patrick saw the man in the mirror as he was closing the medicine cabinet. His breath left him and his blood chilled. "Holy shit, Steven! You scared the hell out of me."

The man didn't seem fazed by Walsh's reaction. "You going somewhere, Lizard? Taking a trip?"

Walsh thought about the Beretta, glad he had loaded it before dropping it into his pocket.

"I thought it would be a good idea. You know, lay low for a while."

Steven nodded. "Where you headed?"

"Not sure. I'll figure it out when I'm on the road."

Steven Jacoby wrapped his right arm snug around the younger man, and stared at their reflections in the mirror. "Now I can't help but ask myself, Lizard..."

"Yeah?"

"Why would you want to leave before I got you your money?"

Walsh didn't know what to say. He needed a good answer, something Jacoby would believe. "I know you'll see to it I get what's coming to me, man. I'm not worried about the cash. I was only thinking being gone a week or two. Right? That's about it."

A large grin sprouted on Jacoby's face, then he began laughing.

"What's the joke, man? What's so funny?"

"Just something you said. It's nothing."

Walsh stared at the mirror, tried to read Jacoby's face. The look in the older man's eyes frightened him. Once again, he thought about the gun in his pocket.

"Finish packing your stuff. I'll take you wherever you want to go."

"You don't have to do that, man."

"I know I don't." Jacoby pulled away from Lizard, put his hand on the side of Lizard's neck in a friendly gesture.

Walsh tried to smile. "All right, then. Thanks."

They rode in Jacoby's Crown Vic for several minutes in silence. "Where we going?" Walsh asked.

Jacoby didn't answer him right away.

"We need to make a stop first. Don't worry, I'll take you wherever you want to go." Jacoby glanced toward the young man. "You want your money, don't you? I'm gonna get it for you now."

They were heading up Mulholland Highway.

Walsh kept glancing around, not sure what he was hoping to see.

Jacoby stopped on the loop of road directly beneath the Hollywood sign.

Walsh peered out the windows—nothing but trees and bushes.

"We meeting someone here or something?" Walsh asked.

Jacoby glanced at his watch. "We're a little early."

An uncomfortable silence filled the cabin of the large sedan.

Jacoby opened the door and climbed out. "Come on, Lizard. Let's take a walk, get some fresh air while we're waiting."

Patrick Walsh climbed slowly from the car, eyed Jacoby suspiciously.

"Come on." Jacoby tilted his head back and took in a deep breath. "It always relaxes me to walk along the trails up here, clear my mind, flush out all the bullshit life tries to bury us under."

"If you say so."

"What? You think a little exercise might kill you?" Another glance at his watch. "We have a few minutes. Come on."

They walked away from the road in silence.

Walsh thought about the Beretta in his pocket. He had a bad feeling about this. If he got the chance, he needed to take it. Something about the look on Jacoby's face.

After a couple of minutes, Jacoby stopped and looked up the side of the hill. "Look up at the sign, Lizard. See it?"

Walsh glanced up the side of Mount Lee. How could he draw his gun without Jacoby noticing?

Jacoby said, "You know, when it was first erected back in 1923, it said HOLLYWOODLAND."

"Really? I didn't know that."

"It was intended as a giant billboard, can you believe that? The brainchild of some wealthy real estate developer."

"That's fascinating," Walsh said, not trying to mask the sarcasm in his voice. He made a show of looking up the side of the mountain, toward the sign, left hand shading the sun from his eyes. He slowly reached into his right pocket and slid his index finger along the gun's side until it sat above the trigger. Jacoby was talking but Walsh couldn't make out the words. Blood pulsed through his head and dulled his sense of hearing.

Walsh swung around and raised the gun, preparing to shoot Steven Jacoby.

Jacoby's larger pistol was already aimed at his head.

"What are you—?"

"You fucked up, Lizard. You fucked up real good."

"W-wait." Walsh lifted his left hand, then looked down at the incriminating gun in his hand. He tossed the weapon to the ground.

"I can fix this, Steven. Come on, man, give me a chance."

Jacoby shook his head. "It's not going to be that easy this time."

"Trust me, man. I can fix it."

"I don't think so, Lizard."

"You don't wanna do this, Steven."

Jacoby smirked at the wiry young man. "They found your fingerprints on the girl's cell phone."

"That's not possible."

"Forensics don't lie, Lizard. It was a clean match. Twenty points."

Walsh shook his head. "Let me think a minute. There's gotta be a way around this."

"You don't understand. It's only a matter of time before someone puts two and two together and starts looking at me for this. I need to get ahead of it while I still can."

"Please don't do this, Steven. I can make it up to you."

"It's too late for that, Lizard. You had one simple job. Just make the call and get Laswell out to the bottom of the river." A beat. "Simple. But then you go and leave your prints on the girl's phone."

"Let me fix this, Steven."

"I don't think so, Lizard."

And Jacoby pulled the trigger.

Two months after the shooting...

Kate Laswell stood in the middle of Laurie's bedroom, and stared at all the pictures she had pinned on her wall. For her thirteenth birthday, they'd given Laurie a wireless photo print-er. The girl had run out of photo paper in less than a day.

Laswell walked up behind his wife. After several silent minutes, he asked, "You all right? What are you looking at?"

Kate removed a photograph from the wall and studied it. It was one of Kate's favorite pictures of Laurie and her father. Laurie, dressed and made up for her first-ever school dance, was standing with Laswell in front of the fireplace. Laurie looked like this was possibly the happiest day of her life. Bill looked as though he were about to be forced to navigate frightening, uncharted waters.

"I didn't want her to ever grow up," Laswell said.

"Why hasn't an arrest been made?" Kate asked. "I need to know that the man responsible has been caught."

"I wish it were that easy, Kate. I really do." He hated to admit what he was about to tell her, what he *had* to tell her. Sometimes the truth is the last thing a person wanted to hear, whether they realized it or not. "We may never make an arrest, Kate." He swallowed. "With each passing day the likelihood grows slimmer and slimmer. You should be prepared for that outcome."

"I need this," Kate said. "I need closure."

Laswell placed his hand on his wife's shoulder. He wanted to hold her, but he sensed that wasn't what she needed right now. "No one ever really gets closure, Kate. It sounds good in theory, but it doesn't exist. No amount of understanding will help you make any sense out of it. There's nothing at all that will make the hurting stop. *Never.* It might become more manageable over time, dull to a quiet ache, but it will always be there."

Laswell let his words hang between them. He didn't know what else he could tell her. Instead, he stared at the photograph in Kate's hand.

"I miss you so much," she said.

Laswell stood in the belly of the concrete river with the blue murder book in his hands. He crouched down like a baseball catcher, set the book on the ground in front of him and then, opened it to the first page of crime scene photographs. One by one, he flipped through the pages, carefully studying each image. There had to be something here, something he had missed before.

He felt the biting chill of early-morning, the rain in his hair, wetness heavy on his coat. He heard the hiss of rubber gliding over slick pavement, and it was suddenly dark. It was night. It was *that* night. The last photo he looked at didn't make sense. What he saw was all wrong...*had* to be. But when he looked down to study the picture more closely, it was gone. Both the photograph and the murder book...*gone.*

Bill Laswell was alone again, alone in the cold wet early-morning hours. Another car passed above on the Olympic Boulevard bridge. One hundred yards away, his daughter was bound to the large wooden pallet.

"Laurie," Laswell shouted. He sprinted toward his daughter, no longer caring about being cautious. Maybe if he got to her fast enough he could save her this time.

But when he reached his daughter, he didn't see a frightened young girl clinging to the hope that her father would arrive in time to save her. What he saw was what had been depicted on the crime scene photograph in the murder book. Laurie's lifeless body hung from the wooden pallet, arms and legs secured to it with black zip ties, face bloodied and bruised. She had been beaten before she died. Her words from that night filled Laswell's ears. *Daddy, I'm sorry.*

But it wasn't her voice he heard—it was his own. In his moment of realization, unable to accept the truth, he had tried to convince himself that it wasn't true. He told himself he could still save her; they still had a chance.

After the first shot rang out, Laswell, realizing he'd been hit, turned to search for the source of the gunfire. He hadn't known he'd been followed, never expected his emotional attachment to the situation would make him so careless.

Lieutenant Lewis had been right.

"I fucked up," Laswell admitted.

"Yes, you did."

Laswell recognized that voice. He glanced around, looking for the speaker.

Steven Jacoby stepped out from behind the support pillar. "Sorry it has to go down like this, partner."

"Why, Steven? Can you tell me that?" Laswell glanced over at his daughter's lifeless body. Then: "Why did you have to kill her? She had nothing to do with any of this."

"I needed to make sure you came out here alone. I needed

to make sure you weren't thinking straight. If you weren't distracted by fear and anger, you might have realized this was a set-up."

"You didn't have to kill her for that."

"I swear to you, partner, that wasn't the plan."

Laswell struggled to say something, but the words died in his throat.

"If she had just cooperated," Jacoby said, "maybe she'd still be alive. But she fought back. She used some moves I can only assume you taught her."

He had, and Laswell now imagined Laurie not going down without a fight.

"I only intended to subdue her to get her under control."

"I'll see to it that you spend the rest of your life in a dark, cold prison cell, Steven. You can count on that."

"I don't think it's gonna work out that way," Jacoby said.

"Count on it, partner. You're lucky I don't simply end your sad, pathetic life right here and now."

Laswell tried to take a deep breath, but couldn't. He moved to wipe perspiration from his forehead, wincing at the pain from his gut.

Jacoby laughed. "Look at you," he said, indicating the bullet wound in Laswell's abdomen. "I don't think you're going to be seeing too much of anything."

"Maybe," Laswell said.

"You should have just looked the other way, partner. Maybe none of us would be here right now."

"You know I couldn't do that, Steven. No one is above the law, not even a cop. Not even my partner."

"Maybe you could have saved your daughter; maybe you could have even saved yourself. It didn't have to go this way."

"Tell yourself what you have to, Steven."

"So long, partner." Jacoby lifted his gun and shot Laswell twice more.

* * *

Kate Laswell answered the knock at the door and found Steven Jacoby standing on her porch. A spark of hope brightened the darkness that had haunted her since the night her daughter and husband had been murdered. "Please tell me you're here with news, Steven."

"Can I come in?"

She led him to the kitchen. Over coffee, she grilled her husband's partner for information.

Is it finally over? Have you made an arrest? Can I finally say goodbye?

Jacoby looked down at his hands before finally lifting his face and looking at the new widow. "It isn't good, Kate. But I wanted you to hear it from me before the media gets ahold of it and starts painting an ugly picture of Bill. He was a good cop, a good father, he doesn't deserve what they're probably going to do to him...do to his memory."

"Oh, God," Kate said. "I don't think I want to hear this, but I know I have to."

Silence filled the room until Jacoby sighed, then said, "Bill got mixed up with some bad people; he was involved in some really ugly shit."

"No," Kate said, her voice a little more than a whisper. "Bill would never do anything like that. He was the most honest person I've ever known."

"I didn't want to believe it either, Kate. I'm so sorry."

"It has to be a mistake," she insisted. "I knew Bill better than anyone. It's why I fell in love with him."

"Once the last piece of the puzzle fell into place, it all came together. There's no avoiding it now."

Kate set herself down on a bar stool, mentally preparing herself for what she didn't want to believe. *Couldn't* believe.

"Bill recognized the voice on the phone that night, and he knew what he had gotten himself mixed up in had ultimately put Laurie in danger."

"I don't understand," Kate admitted.

"Bill was going to turn himself in, face the consequences of his actions. He was finally planning to do the right thing. But Lizard couldn't let that happen. He knew he would have gone down with Bill. He knew he wouldn't survive being sent back to prison. He was desperate. He had to do something."

"You need to slow down, Steven." She paused, then asked, "Who's Lizard? What are you talking about?"

"Patrick Walsh. Known on the street as Lizard. I did some digging. Bill was using him as a confidential informant. That's probably how he got mixed up in everything to begin with."

"It doesn't make any sense. What was Bill supposedly mixed up in?"

Jacoby frowned. "It's still an ongoing investigation, Kate. I shouldn't even be here telling you what I'm telling you. But I wanted the news to come from me."

"I appreciate that, Steven. I do." She shook her head. "So this Lizard person. Has he been arrested? Is that what you came to tell me?"

"He's dead," Jacoby told her. Blunt, all business. "Shot himself to death. He left a suicide note explaining everything. How and why. It's a very detailed note. It directs us to a very condemning paper trail which clearly implicates Bill."

"You saw the note?"

"Yes."

"He admitted to killing Laurie?"

"He admitted to killing them both."

Kate began to cry.

Jacoby moved closer to her, placed his arm around her, gently pulled her close to him. "It's over, Kate."

She wept and cried into Jacoby's chest, grateful for her husband's partner. She pulled away and whispered, "I'm sorry, Steven. None of this seems real."

"I understand," Jacoby said. "It's perfectly all right."

Kate Laswell stepped away from Jacoby, and announced, "Bill's been here."

"*What?*"

"The past few days. I've felt him, his presence. It was as if he had something he needed to tell me. Unfinished business."

"You're serious?"

"Yes. And based on what you've just shared with me, maybe he was trying to tell me he was sorry for what he had done."

"Maybe," Jacoby agreed.

Kate stared at her husband's partner for a long moment. "Or maybe he was sorry for what he had *allowed* to happen."

"I don't understand. What do you mean?"

"I can't explain it," Kate admitted. "I'm not sure I fully understand all this 'afterlife' stuff. But...I *talked* to him."

"You talked to him?"

"I told him I was mad at him, that I was trying not to hate him."

"That's understandable, Kate. You're angry. You're hurt. You feel as though he abandoned you, as though he failed Laurie."

She nodded. "Yes. You're right. You *were*. But I was wrong."

"Wrong about what?"

"Maybe I was wrong about all of it. I *felt* him. It was *real*. When I was standing in Laurie's bedroom, he placed his hand on my shoulder. I was afraid to breathe, afraid to move. I was afraid to break the connection we had. I swear I could even smell his aftershave. And then he spoke to me."

"It's what you wanted to believe, Kate. Your mind playing tricks on you, telling you what you wanted more than anything to hear."

"Maybe you're right, Steven. But I know what I felt, and I know what I heard. It was real. The energy in the room...it was the same energy that was always there when Bill was angry, when he was determined."

"I'm sure it must have felt that way. But it was just what

you wanted, what you *needed* to feel. It's normal, Kate. It's a form of coping mechanism."

"Maybe. Or maybe not. He *spoke* to me."

"Kate, don't. You're not—"

"It happened more than once." She took a slow breath. "I was in the kitchen, at the sink doing dishes. Bill was there with me. I felt him. I didn't turn to look because I needed to feel him there with me; I didn't want him to leave me again."

Jacoby opened his mouth to speak, but Kate said, "I was angry. I was reminding him that he had promised me he would never let anything happen to Laurie. I don't know, I guess I wanted him to know how much I was hurting."

"I'm sure he knows, Kate."

"I know you're right. Just like I know he didn't do what you claim he did."

"I wish it wasn't true, I swear I do. But the evidence doesn't lie."

A familiar chill moved through Kate. She fought back the urge to glance around the room—they were no longer alone. And she didn't want to let on to Jacoby that she was beginning to learn the real truth. She could feel Bill's worry and concern. And then he spoke to her.

He isn't going to hurt you, Kate. Don't be afraid. I won't let him do anything to you, I promise. He thinks he thought of everything; he thinks he's going to get away with all of it. But that isn't going to happen. What he just said about evidence against me was all a lie. There is evidence. I know, because I'm the one who compiled it. He thought killing me would get him off the hook...but he was wrong. Get rid of him now, Kate. Tell him to leave. And once he's gone, I'll show you where I had been keeping all the evidence. You can take it to Lieutenant Lewis. She'll know what to do with it.

"I think it's time for you to leave, Steven," Kate blurted. "I don't want you in my home any longer."

Jacoby cocked his head. "What are you talking about?"

"I told you, Steven. I *heard* him. Bill *talked* to me. At first I thought I'd imagined it, that I had wanted it so badly that I simply made it up. But I didn't. He was here, he spoke to me."

Jacoby smirked. "Okay, okay, fine. What did he say?"

"He said he was going to find the bastard who did this. He said he was going to make him pay."

Jacoby just stared at her.

"Bill's trying to make things right," Kate continued. "He feels guilty because of what he *didn't* do not because of what he *did*. He failed to save his daughter, he failed to save himself. I think he even believes he failed me somehow. He won't be able to rest until he gets to the bottom of what really happened that night. You know how relentless he can be. He'll figure it out. I know he will. Maybe he already has." She nodded. A nearly imperceptible movement. "Either way, someone will have hell to pay."

THE FUNNEL OF LOVE
Cyndra Gernet

May 5, 1934

"Two bucks a night," said the old man behind the desk at the Ride-in Motor Court somewhere on the jagged edges of Los Angeles. Pelum Thomas fingered the few coins inside the pocket of his overalls. He wouldn't have to pay until check out. He'd figure something out before then.

"Number six." With a gnarled hand, the clerk in the tiny front office snagged a key from a half-filled rack and stretched it toward Pelum. As he reached out, the key clattered onto the counter.

"Sorry," said the clerk. He settled himself more firmly on the padded stool and pointed out the window.

Pelum opened the office door and scooted out into the balmy night air. He maneuvered his battered Nash sedan into the room-side garage, grabbed a satchel from the back seat and entered his room. The décor was attempted Western; maple headboard with twisted rope detail and matching nightstand. The chenille bedspread featured a cowboy twirling a straw-colored lasso. The theme petered out at the dresser, which was standard-issue brown.

Pelum flopped onto the bed, twisted his hands beneath his head, and stared at the ceiling. What in hell was he going to do? His stomach, long past growling, tweaked with hunger. Too busy driving, he hadn't eaten in two days. Seeking shelter had seemed more important than food, but now...

He grabbed the room key, locked up, and walked down the road to the nearby restaurant he had passed minutes before.

Approaching a building shaped like a train car, Pelum blinked at the bright pink neon sign proclaiming The RR Diner. Inside a scatter of customers sat in yellow plastic booths arranged under the picture windows of the café to simulate train seats. He circled around back of the diner and paused at the kitchen's open screen door.

An angry male voice floated on a whiff of smoky air. "You son-of-a-bitch, you don't know what you're doing. You said you could cook. Those burgers are charred, and you're behind on the orders." The man speaking gave the order wheel a vicious spin. Pelum couldn't make out the softer voice.

"Well you better catch on fast, or I'll fire your ass."

Pelum cleared his throat and raised a fist to knock.

Two faces turned and stared. One was angry red and towered above the other. "What do *you* want?" said the taller man, eyeing Pelum's wiry frame covered in worn overalls.

"Food in exchange for helping you cook. I've worked short order for years." Pelum looked in the other face and saw alarm rising in the small man's eyes. "Don't want your job, I'm just hungry. Can I come in?"

"Looks like you're in already. Name's Wilson." The big man moved forward extending his hand. As he shook Pelum's, he gripped it hard. "Teach idiot Sam here something quick. I got customers waiting."

Wilson barged through the swinging doors into the restaurant.

Pelum turned to the other man, who was now moving meat around on the grill. "Know anything about cooking?"

Sam grinned. "Not much. But I am a fast learner."

"Then we can learn together."

Sam's grin widened.

Hours later, Sam and Pelum had caught up on the orders without burning a single meal. In between peeling twenty-five pounds of potatoes for frying and grilling dozens of burgers and dogs, Pelum had eaten his fill. The door closed on the last customer with a bang, and the men heard Wilson lock up. While he cleaned the dining room, they settled the kitchen.

Sam pushed a wet mop along the tile floor as he eyed Pelum. "You must have done some cooking somewhere."

"Just burgers and dogs." Pelum reached for the metal scraper and began cleaning the griddle. "How about you?"

"I cook for my family only. I needed the job bad. I had to lie. He'd never have hired me if I hadn't."

"I hear you. Lying is a necessary skill these days." Pelum slid the scummy cooked residue from the scraper into a blue Maxwell House coffee can and continued cleaning the grill. "I've had use of it myself many times."

"Where you come from, then?" Sam was circling the kitchen skirting the spot in front of the stove where Pelum stood.

Pelum hesitated. Should he keep quiet or tell his tale? He'd driven steady from the far side of Arizona, the story clawing at his back like a wet cat. "There a bar around here?" he asked.

"Sure, there's the Lost Cause up the road a ways."

Pelum turned around, the grill finished. "Great name. Got time for a beer?"

The bar was half full. Voices and cigarette smoke filled the air. Pelum could just hear the notes of *Chattanooga Choo Choo* coming from the corner jukebox. He and Sam settled at a table near the window.

Sam pulled a pack of smokes from his pocket, shook out two, lit one. He slid the lighter to Pelum.

Pelum rolled the cigarette between his fingers. A waitress appeared, her middle-aged body clad in an aproned uniform designed for a younger woman. She slapped down thick paper coasters and removed a pencil from her rolled hairdo. "What'll it be, gentlemen?"

Pelum tapped the coaster advertising Budweiser for fifteen cents a bottle. "Two of these." He looked to Sam for confirmation. Sam nodded.

"You eating?" asked the waitress.

"Just the beer."

"Thought so. You don't look like big spenders." She pushed the pencil back into her hair and moved away.

Pelum lit the cigarette and took a long drag.

Sam waited a beat. "Back at the restaurant, you were gonna tell me where you're from."

Pelum set the coaster on edge and gave it a twirl. "I'm from Arizona originally. Grew up there, so I'm used to a hot climate like here." He itched to tell his tale to an eager listener. "But I had to leave in a hurry. I had to run, actually."

Sam quirked an eyebrow and tapped ashes into a notched plastic ashtray.

"I was working Barnaby's Traveling Carnival. We musta hit every Podunk town in the state. That's where I learned to cook, but I did some of everything." Pelum heard nickels drop and *Chattanooga Choo Choo* began playing for the fourth time.

"I started as a backyard boy, doing whatever job didn't take any skill 'cause believe me back then, I had no skills. I was fifteen. I wanted to be a carney just like my pa. The carnival was family to me, never knew another." Pelum ran a hand over his face "I spent ten years on the road working the trade."

"Must of cooked a lot of dogs in that time," Sam said.

"That I did, among other things. Anyway, I worked my way up to where I was a ride monkey. Worked a shake machine for a while."

"A shake machine?"

"Yeah, a ride that emptied the townies' pockets and made them puke." Pelum grinned as Sam pulled a face. "It was messy, but the money was good. My ride, The Kama-Kazi, was a real draw so she stood in the back lot to pull the crowds in. Walt the Philosopher was closer to the mid-way. He ran the Tunnel of Love."

"This guy Walt, he was old?"

"He musta been sixty, at least. He was one of those guys that talk about life all the time, wondering why we're here, what it's all about, not religious but curious. You know?"

"Yep," Sam said. "My pop was kind of like that."

The waitress placed two icy bottles atop the coasters and set the bill on the table. Both men lifted a bottle and took a long drink.

"You guys can pay up now." The waitress stood hand on hip, waiting.

Pelum laid down a quarter and two nickels.

"Aren't you sweet? Not everybody tips on a thirty-cent tab."

She slipped the extra nickel into her pocket. "Enjoy your drink."

"I wish I could go on the road." Sam lifted his beer in a salute. "I've never been out of L.A."

Pelum picked at the label of the bottle, trying to loosen it with his fingernail. "Ah, the traveling life's not for everyone. It will take out of you as much as it puts in, Walt used to say, sometimes more. He had a day a couple of months ago that made him question life on the road."

"Oh, yeah?"

"Yeah. I was cleaning my machine, getting her ready for the crowds when Walt came running up his face twisted funny. 'You gotta see this,' he said. He grabbed the rag out of my hand and pulled me along the lot. When we got to his ride, he pointed up at the opening arch over where the cars go in, and instead of Tunnel of Love, it said Funnel of Love. Some vandal had added an extra line to the T."

Sam nodded his head. "We get a little of that around here, usually on cement walls."

"Well, when Walt sees the word, he thinks it's a sign. Lots of carneys are superstitious. 'Funnel of Love,' he said. 'That's my life. I thought it was a tunnel. I thought I had a shot straight through from birth to death, clean like, but now everything's closing in on me like the narrow end of a funnel.'"

Sam had leaned in to hear better in the noisy bar.

"Walt starts talking and can't stop. It was like he was dying and his whole life was passing before him but in words, not pictures. Best I could make out was that he had wasted his chances, thrown love away, and was riding the Jumbo Slide to the big sleep. Life was closing in on him."

Across the table, Sam stifled a yawn.

Pelum glanced Sam's way, then studied his beer. "Look, what's say we save the rest of this for another day. I'm beat."

Back at the motel, Pelum peeled the chenille cowboy quilt the length of the bed. As the spread moved the air, he caught a whiff of carnival, that unique blend of sweat, popcorn, crushed grass, and oil. He tensed. Had he been followed from Arizona?

Standing still, his eyes swept over the dresser, the nightstand, the rug. They came to rest at his satchel on the floor of the open closet. He crossed the room, lifted the bag, and placed it on the bed. With hands clumsy with nerves, he opened the canvas case. Atop his clothes in red letters on white paper, were the words, "Found You."

Pelum wiped sweaty hands down his pant legs and tried not to panic. Who had come after him? His mind raced through the possibilities. He hoped it wasn't Maco, the Strong Man who could lift grown men off the ground in his massive fists.

Sinking onto the bed, note in hand, Pelum tried to read personality into the printed letters. If the Bearded Lady showed up, no problem, although she was fierce when mad.

Alligator Man would be okay. His skin condition wasn't contagious, and he was kind of puny.

Pelum's thoughts flew back to Walter. Walt had been the closest to a father he'd had for most of his life. Pelum's real dad had been a career carney, and what he hadn't told Sam was that he had died when Pelum was eight. Life before the carnival had been a mix of living rough on the streets or rougher still in state-run orphanages. Just because he'd found Walt's body didn't make him a murderer.

Loud knocking filled the room. His fate stood on the other side of the door.

"Open up, Pelum. We know you're in there."

It was worse than he'd thought. It was the knife thrower, Darryl, whose skills were questionable. Pelum had seen the result of several of his "misses" on the arms and legs of his wife-target, Mildred.

"I'll bust the door down. You know I will."

Oh, great. The Strong Man was with him.

Pelum crossed the room and flung open the door. The Strong Man launched himself into the room, sending Pelum flat onto his back. Before he could right himself, Maco took a seat on his chest. "You ran like the rat you are."

Darryl circled the men rubbing his hands together. "A knife will set him talking." He pulled an eight-inch blade from his belt and waved it around.

"We don't need a knife, idiot." Maco's showy handlebar mustache bobbed as he spoke. "I'll just squeeze the story out of him."

"You're crushing him. He can't talk, hell, he can't breathe."

Pelum took gurgling sips of air and pushed at the weight that held him.

Maco rolled off, pulling Pelum up by his shirt and tossing him onto the bed. "So, talk. What was your beef with Walt? Why'd you kill him?"

Pelum drew deep breaths between words. "I told you before

I left, I didn't kill him."

"You were caught red-handed with his dead body." Maco stood before him, stance wide, arms crossed.

Pelum stood. "He was stuck in the number one car in the Tunnel of Love."

"You're the one put him in there, then you staged pulling him out."

"I was trying to save him. He had a heart condition he was keeping secret. I was looking for his pills. They weren't in his pockets."

Maco shook his head. "He didn't have a heart condition. He was strong for an old man. He always helped with loading and striking the rides."

"He'd be fired if the boss knew so he always pulled his weight, but it cost him." Pelum straightened his shirt. "Somebody killed Walt, but it wasn't me."

Darryl bounced his eyes from man to man. "You believe him, Maco?"

The big man moved to the side of the dresser, nudged the bottom drawer open with his boot and propped a foot on it. "Tell us what happened."

Pelum kept his eyes on Maco. "Okay. Saturday morning, I woke up early and couldn't get back to sleep. I drove to the midway. I got there around four thirty. The place was quiet. The regulars were still asleep. When I passed Lucy's wagon, I heard her snoring."

The three men exchanged a knowing look. The Bearded Lady had a thunderous snore.

"Anyone see you?" Maco asked.

"No. I went straight to my ride. She'd been squealing some the night before. I oiled her joints and checked the engine. You know how all the boys love that one red car with the picture of Buck Rodgers on it? I polished that one 'til it shone like the funhouse mirror. I finished around six. Most of the crew was already working—" he shot Daryl a look, "—but I saw you sneaking out of Pretzel Paula's wagon."

Maco kicked the dresser drawer shut. "You fool. If her husband finds out you've been messing with his meal ticket, you're toast."

Pelum didn't blame Darryl for wanting the contortionist, she was a peach, but he couldn't resist needling him. At a signal from Maco, he continued his tale.

"The cookhouse was open, so I got coffee for me and Walt like usual. When I got to his ride, he wasn't there. He's always in by five-thirty. I got suspicious and started poking around."

"His ride still reads Funnel of Love," Darryl said. "I don't get it. Isn't a funnel a kitchen tool?"

Ignoring Darryl, Pelum continued. "I thought it was a warning, like no matter how far you go you can't escape your fate. Life funnels down to the things you did wrong."

Maco shot Darryl a knowing look. "Yeah, we've all got regrets."

"Then what?" asked Darryl.

"I noticed the flaps at the entrance to the tunnel weren't hanging right. I went in. The cars were lined up like usual. I walked the right-hand ledge. With no flashlight, the farther in I got the less I could see, but I looked in each car. I'd never walked the ride before. It's a lot longer than it looks from the outside."

The two men nodded. They knew the "mystery" rides could feel strange when you weren't a rider.

"The tunnel seemed to grow tighter. At first, I thought it was my nerves, but when I reached car six, I had to hop off the ledge. The walls were angling in."

"Oh, come on." Darryl flapped a hand. "When the cops came, they inspected the ride. It was normal."

"It wasn't when I was in it. The tunnel kept shrinking, the ceiling got lower, the sides grew closer. By the time I reached car three, the ride was the size of a tube, like, well, like the end of a funnel. There was so little room I had to drag myself over the cars. And then I found Walt."

Maco pushed his face close to Pelum's. "Was he alive?"

"He was slumped in the car barely breathing. I searched for the pills he always carried. They weren't there. I was about to go for help when Walt opened his eyes. In the dark, I could only see the whites. I told him he'd be okay; that I'd get the medic."

He put out a hand to stop me. I could hear him breathing. "'Years ago,' he said, 'I killed a man. A carney.' His voice grew weaker. 'He stole my woman.' Walt clutched his chest. 'This is revenge.' His hand fell from my arm. He died right in front of me." Pelum's eyes filled with tears.

"But who killed him?" asked Darryl. "A ghost? His guilty conscience?"

Blinking fast, Pelum stood up, pushed his hands into his pockets. "Walt might have said it was the ride itself, The Funnel of Love."

Uneasy now in the dim room, the three men began to move. Maco pushed away from the dresser. Daryl wiped his hands down his pant legs. Pelum walked to the window.

"Come back with us," said Maco. "We'll make it right."

Pelum stared at the men who were so sure he'd killed Walt they'd chased him to another state. "I don't think so."

He looked out the window at the motel courtyard's single orange tree and breathed in the scent of its blossoms. He'd told the story well, and they'd believed him.

The next day, Pelum knelt on the sun-dappled ground of Pioneer Cemetery. "It's like you always said, Pop, getting revenge is easy. I could have just killed Walt." He shifted a pile of fallen pine needles that obscured a plaque reading Thomas Scott, Beloved Father, Career Carney. "But I didn't want easy. I wanted justice."

Pelum leaned closer to the grave. "With one stroke of paint,

I got old Walt to review his life and to confess to your murder. My turning the tunnel into the Funnel of Love forced him into a heart attack."

Standing up, Pelum brushed dirt from his pants. He smiled down at his father. "Now that's what I call justice."

TICK-TOCK
Lisa Ciarfella

She sat on the corner of the bed and stared at the army of ants climbing single file up the beige bathroom wall from the sticky, vinyl floor. She watched as they claimed even more territory, turning the white countertop tile a dark shade of gray. Lulu had been holed up in the city of Angels just three days now, and room 209 at the Lucky Lickety-Split Motel was feeling anything but lucky.

Exactly what the joint was lucky for, she couldn't say. But if she had a prize for Most Seedy Motel, she'd give it. And it all felt so familiar too. Not because she'd been there before—she hadn't. But because the place reminded her of all the similar low-rent spaces she'd clawed her way out of back home in the South before busting out of town with Sammy. Dirty by-the-hour places for rent, hostels, and dingy wood-paneled bars, all lined up like Legos and scattered throughout Atlanta, Austin, and Louisiana. Street after street, littered with the same empty bottles of cheap booze and beer cans, and the endless sound of chained up dogs barking furiously into the night. Places she'd been unlucky enough to call home, and dives in which she'd slung countless beers to survive. And from what little she'd seen so far, L.A. was no different. Maybe even worse.

The stench of desperation was everywhere. Take that odd downtown dive Sammy took her to their first night in town, dishing out meals to the luckless souls haunting skid row. It was there Lulu saw more than she'd cared to, between the pans of greasy meatloaf and the small bowls of Jell-O for dessert. In the bathroom, she'd nearly stumbled over a junkie shooting up on the worn, black and white linoleum floor. They should have blown this town already. The fact that she was still here set her teeth on a permanent grind.

Lulu watched the ants climb higher, and still, the phone didn't ring. *Call now, damn it, Sammy*, she willed to the silent telephone. Hot tears welled up and streaked down the smooth, even sides of her face. She'd been waiting on him a good six hours and forty-nine minutes, but who was counting? On the opposite wall, she spied Felix the Cat hanging low, his big mechanical hands ticking time down fast, and those hours came and went. Just like that.

Last night's plan had been simple. Lulu, Sammy, and Trevor should have rendezvoused back here after boosting as many pieces as possible from the L.A. Convention Center's 1983 Annual International Gem and Jewelry show. It was why they'd come to town. Sammy's latest, and supposed last, get-rich scheme.

The show was crammed to the rafters, filled with all the sparkly diamonds, gemstones, and estate jewelry a girl could dream about. The perfect place for a grab 'n' go, Sammy's version of dine 'n' dash, a game Lulu played a lot growing up. Her family, too poor to eat out, had scammed meals at the local slop shops by flying out the door seconds after the waitress dropped the check. Those checks never got paid.

Having spent most of her life waiting on others, bailing on tabs was no longer Lulu's game. She knew all too well what it was like to scrape by on tips.

She'd spent her late teens and most of her twenties running back and forth in sky-high-heels along the Thirsty Dog's hard, beer-stained floor. She dealt with those clients, those fat men with bad breath and sticky fingers, who continually tried to stick them where they didn't belong. Lulu never danced like the other girls, but she was contemplating making that move. At least those girls made enough to pay their rent. Then Sammy slugged into the bar.

She poured him his Schlitz malt as he watched Trina climb the greasy pole onstage for the nine hundred and ninety-thousandth time. Suddenly, Sammy reached over and grabbed Lulu's hand. His lips brushed close against her ear.

"Babe, those girls dancin' up there, they're nothing but money grabbing hos. I got a knack for telling, and I can tell you're not like that. Don't try to deny it now."

As if she heard, Trina, the club's top grosser shimmied by, winking her big black falsies and shaking her waist-length, lustrous blonde mane back and forth. She pointed a long, blood red manicured finger towards Sammy, and motioned towards the private rooms.

"Meet you in the back in five, sugar, and bring lots of cash. You know we always have ourselves a real good time."

Even Lulu had to admit, Trina's ass, flanked in a flossie the size of a straw, looked pretty damn good. Fully expecting Sammy to follow the dancer, she was surprised when he stayed put.

"Hey, Trina," Sammy called out. "You're looking sharp and all, but our dancing days are over. I got what I want. And it's right here."

Draping an arm around Lulu's shoulders, he'd pulled her close. He stood just a hint over five feet tall. She wasn't too sure yet if Sammy meant what he'd said, but it sounded good to her. Good enough to overlook that funny limp on his right side and the fact that he was nearly a decade older.

Sammy had been good on his word. He'd show up and pay the house for her shift so Lulu wouldn't have to run on her heels all night long. And when she was short on rent, he'd make that happen too. Lulu could have picked worse. Finally, a caring man had come into her life.

After they'd hooked up, Sammy taught her the ropes on some of his scams. He'd grown up stealing stuff at dime stores while he distracted clerks with magic tricks. He'd learned to do this by watching his dad, a fledgling magician, perform at local carnival shows. As time passed Sammy moved on to bigger takes, like electronics and jewelry. He convinced Lulu to help him pull one last job in L.A. "We'll score enough to quit running," he told her. "Then we'll settle down somewhere nice. Just us two."

And she'd believed him.

For this last job, Sammy wanted Lulu to play eye-candy to distract, while he got busy with the take. He needed her best assets dressed to kill, up front and center. Although the two of them worked as a pair, Sammy wanted additional help because the gem show offered too many goodies to pass up. He asked a local L.A. con named Trevor to join them.

Trevor was waiting for them at The Pantry, a famous L.A. diner, the second night after the Greyhound dumped them into town. Sporting an over-sized charcoal-black trench, scuffed up combat boots, and plenty of hardware to match, Trevor seemed out of place in the landmark eatery. A pock-marked twenty-something, his face spelled trouble.

"You Trevor?" Sammy cautioned as they approached the young man sitting alone in the cracked, orange leatherette booth near the rear of the restaurant. Seriously working on a plate of scrambled 'n' hash, the punk barely glanced up. The whole runny mess looked to Lulu like the cooks had fried it up from eggs older than the joint itself.

"Yeah, man, that's me," he mumbled, mouthing through sausage. "You're Sammy, right? Christ-almighty, Jack said you were short but damn! Anyway, look, I wasn't expecting you for another hour, so sit down and order up. Might as well since you'll be picking up the check."

He grinned as he sawed through his eggs and checked out Lulu.

"Who's the babe?" he said, leaning over to get a better view of Lulu's cleavage.

Wrapped up tight in a tiny, low cut blouse because that's how Sammy liked it, Lulu bristled for a hot second but shook it off. She'd dealt with guys like Trevor before.

"This is Lulu. Lulu, Trevor." Sammy leaned in for eye contact. "You come highly recommended from my guys back home. They said you've got legendary lifting skills." He motioned to a waitress, who whizzed by fast.

"I hope your lifting's cleaner than your eating." Lulu pointed to the blood-orange salsa dribbling slowly down the front of Trevor's trench, leaving grease stains the same color as the booth beneath. He looked down, smirked and sopped up the mess with a greasy napkin.

"Don't worry your sexy little legs about that none, babe. I get the job done." He shifted back toward Sammy. "You know what I charge, right? A hundred up front, call it a goodwill gesture on your part. And half the take after." He crunched toast and devoured Lulu with his eyes. "So. You want me, or not?"

"Job's big," Sammy told him. "Way bigger than we can handle. So yeah, I need your help. And Lulu here's our lookout. Our decoy. She'll make sure they look the other way when we come 'round, if you catch my drift."

Trevor caught it but good. He licked his chops, stared at Lulu, and nodded.

"Meet us out front of the convention center at six o'clock sharp tomorrow night. We grab what we can and get out quick. After, we meet up at the Lucky Lickety-Split, room 209. If we get split up, plan's the same. Lucky Lickety-Split."

A plump server with a nametag that read Martha dumped more coffee in Trevor's cup and asked Sammy and Lulu if they wanted anything.

"We're done here," Sammy told her. "But thanks anyway."

Martha smiled the mandatory server smile. Lulu knew it well, having used it a million times back home. The waitress dropped the check in front of Trevor, who pushed it in front of Sammy. With a grunt, Sammy plopped down two Jacksons, face down. Lulu had seen him do that a lot because he had a thing about bills. Never liked the president's eyes looking up at him. Gave him the creeps.

Standing up, Sammy grabbed Lulu's hand. "My guy said you were good. Just hope he was right. But I don't pay till the job's done. Period. If you can't slide down that coaster, we can't roll."

Trevor eyed Sammy. Waited a beat.

"Yeah, okay. I guess I can wait. But only because Jack hooked us up." Crunching burnt toast hard, he swallowed even harder. Sammy yanked Lulu toward the door.

"Hey, babe!" Trevor shouted loud enough for heads to turn two booths over. "Do me a favor and wear that top tomorrow. It's doing wonders for my imagination!"

He whistled low and long, a bulldog waiting on his bone. Lulu felt his eyes burrowing into her calves as Sammy pulled her outside.

At the Lucky Lickety-Split, Lulu watched the ant trail grow full tilt, just like that creep, Trevor. Both disgusting. But Trevor was the least of her worries. Right now, she was more worried about Sammy. It was going on nine hours and twenty-six minutes, and still no sign of either of them. They should have been here by now, she told the insects. But the ants paid no mind and kept on marching. Felix the Cat kept on ticking.

Lulu stretched out on the bed, musing over last night's job.

It started out well but quickly turned sour once they'd reached their prime target, the Thai American Gems booth, which specialized in precious Bangkok stones. Stones were easy for Sammy to pawn, given his connections back home. And that's where he'd wanted to do the most damage.

At the show, Sammy and Trevor had warmed up good, with quite a few smalls from the less impressive booths. Things like mineral rocks, crystals, and chains. When Lulu reached the targeted booth, she kicked her act into high gear, leaning over the counter to make good use of her new low-cut tank. Showing off her wares to their finest points, she nearly spilled out completely, making it hard not to notice her "assets."

She aimed her best sweet eyes straight at the goateed young kid standing behind the table display. Her candy-cane-colored thigh-high mini and stilettos drew him in with laser-like precision, even though the booth was packed.

"Wow, these necklaces are sooo pretty," Lulu murmured, pretending to be all thumbs with the trinkets on display. "Any chance I can try one on, just for a second? Could you help me with the clasp?"

The booth was busy with Japanese businessmen and gawking tourists, all perusing the merchandise and swapping business cards. Everyone wanted something, but the goatee-guy only had eyes for Lulu.

"You bet, honey. Let me come around and give you a hands-on tutorial."

He grunted delightedly as he moved his substantial frame out from behind the display. Sammy, who'd been watching from a distance, made his move. Using his most perfected sleight of hand trick, he swooshed an entire row of large sapphires and opals into his convention goody bag. Beside him, Trevor did the same with a row of rubies and estate rings, tucking them deep inside his trench pockets. Lulu was doing a good job keeping the kid busy when, out of the corner of her eye, she spied a tall girl with jet-black hair and glasses, videotaping the whole thing on one of those new, smart look-ing camcorders. The woman wore a pinstriped suit, which made Lulu think the woman taped the booth for business rea-sons. Whatever the reason, this was a big problem.

Waving her arms, she motioned for Sammy to run. Trevor picked up on the cue and took off like a racehorse down the center aisle, knocking over a trashcan as he went. As far as Lulu could tell, he made it out clean. But Sammy's mug had been caught on video for sure. Lulu panicked and whipped around, planting her cleavage smack into the middle of the goatee-guy's face.

"Show me again how you clasp this. I just can't get the hang of it."

She saw Sammy take off, but not before knocking over the camera girl and sending her sprawling into the display case. The girl in the suit slid to the floor and dropped the camcorder, which skittered toward Sammy. He spotted it, grabbed it, and ran. When the girl adjusted her glasses and tried to rise again, Lulu pretended to trip on her heels and fell into the girl, send-ing her sprawling back down again.

"Oh my gosh, I'm such a klutz! Are you all right?"

The girl searched the ground frantically for her camera.

"Hey, did you see those guys? They took a bunch of jewelry and stuff. I got it all on video, but I think one of 'em grabbed my camcorder!"

As Lulu watched the girl search hunt for her camcorder, she felt a split-second of deja vu. Before she could form a thought, goatee-guy jumped between the two women.

"You're not hurt, are you? What the hell!" He took in the scene, craning his head back and forth between the girls and his ruined display. "What a freakin' mess! Security!"

He stood in the middle of the aisle and pumped his arms up and down. "Someone call security. I just got robbed!" He turned to Lulu and the black-haired girl. "Can either of you identify the guys? You both got a good look, right?"

"Uh—no, I can't," Lulu said. "It all happened so fast." Her eyes surveyed the area, looking for signs of Sammy or Trevor. There were none.

"I can," shouted the black-haired girl. "The guy who took my camcorder wore a bright red jacket and looked really young; just a kid, I think."

That's odd, thought Lulu. Her description didn't fit either Trevor or Sammy. But then she realized it was better this way. Lulu turned back to the goatee-guy, whose nametag she now saw read Chuck.

"Yeah, I think she's right, Chuck." To the girl, she said, "Sorry I made you fall."

"No problem." The girl smoothed her black hair.

Again, déjà vu.

Several security guys in navy blue sports coats and badges hustled towards them. It set her wheels spinning. Lulu needed to get out quick. The men arrived, walkie-talkies in hand, and cleared the path both in front and behind the booth. Before they could question her, Lulu edged into the crowd and sprinted off.

Outside the convention hall, she looked for Sammy but didn't see him. She hailed a cab with a shaky hand and directed the driver to go to the Lucky Lickety-Split. What should have been a five-minute drive turned into twenty, which didn't help her nerves any. As the driver weaved his way snail-like through L.A. evening traffic, Lulu closed her eyes and thought about The Thirsty Dog, the bar where she'd first met Sammy. A low-life place filled to the rafters with scoundrels and skull-crackers. She hung onto Sammy's pronouncement of love.

"Just this one big score in L.A., and I'll set you up fine, Lulu. You'll see."

* * *

Brrrrrriiinng...Brrrrriiiinng...Brrrrrrriiiinng...

The ringing jolted Lulu out of her haze. She reached over and grabbed the phone quick.

"Yes?" she whispered into the mouthpiece. "Sammy, that you?"

"Hell, no," Trevor screeched. "Better brace yourself, babe. I don't know where that scumbag is, but I'm pretty sure he double-crossed us both. Saw him run out of the convention center not ten minutes after I did. I yelled, but he ignored me and waved down a car parked on the other side of the street. Some smoking hot blonde was driving it."

Lulu swallowed hard, a lump forming in her throat. He went on.

"The blonde stuck her head out the window and yelled for Sammy to dump everything in the trunk. When I caught up, he yelled for me to do the same, so I did. Threw in my stash, and then the car peeled out without me."

Lulu stayed quiet. Stared hard at the ants. Tried to breathe.

"You still there, babe? I know it sucks. I ran after them but couldn't keep up. Lost 'em once they passed the Hotel Figueroa." He laughed. "A high rollers joint, that place. Worked there parking fancy cars in high school until they fired me for trying to steal one." He chuckled again at his bravado. "Too bad, too. Tips were always great. Guess good gigs die hard."

Lulu wanted to scream.

"Uh, another thing, I think the bitch driving was the one filming us. You know, the girl he knocked over. Sammy called her Tina or Trina. Something like that."

Trina? Lulu's eyes went wide. She remembered that twinge of familiarity when she knocked the girl over at the booth. Half dazed, she listened as Trevor continued.

"I thought I'd hunt the two of them down, but since she got each of us on video, I think it's best to steer clear. You should, too. Sammy's a weasel all right, and I wouldn't put it past him to use that tape against us if we push him. Sorry, babe."

Lulu's body sank lower on the bed.

"I guess Sammy screwed us both, but I've lived in this town long enough to see worse. His scam's kind of regular in L.A." He paused, and then said, "But, hey, I managed to keep a little something in my jacket. Why don't you let me take you out on the town? You know, as a consolation prize...What do you say, babe?"

Lulu had nothing to say.

"Forget about that lowlife...he's too old for you anyway. And he's definitely got alternate plans, which don't seem to include you. Come on. Let me cheer you up. Meet me over at El Compadre, my favorite bar in town. The place has wicked Mexican food, and the bartender's a buddy of mine who makes a mean banana daiquiri. What do you say?"

Lulu dragged herself into a seated position. Wicked. Mean. She'd always had bad luck with men. Why should Sammy be any different?

"See you in an hour," she said. Lulu hung up the phone and hung her head.

At the Biltmore Hotel, Trevor set the phone down. It was one of those expensive looking models, white, with black porcelain keys and a fancy round dial pad. The Biltmore could afford to treat their guests well, and he was already eyeing one of those deluxe plush bathrobes hanging in the closet to take as a token.

"So, how'd I do?" He turned to look at Sammy, who eyed him carefully as he laid out the gems on the bed. "Was I convincing enough for you?"

Sammy shrugged his shoulders and labeled the stones. Some were worth a bloody fortune, and Trevor had never seen so much sparkle up close before.

"You were perfect," Sammy said. "Lulu will never know

what really went down. Best part is, we get to split her share."

"You need to pay me my cut now so I can get lost, you know?" Trevor exhaled. "Man, I know it's none of my business, but that was cold."

Sammy shrugged again and cast his eyes over at Trina, spread out on the couch like she owned the place and sucking down an Old Fashioned. Her ultra-thick, long blonde mane cascaded over her shoulders to her waist, the ends just grazing a black wig and glasses sitting on top of a cashmere pillow. She raised her glass in a toast to Sammy. He shot her a quick thumbs-up.

"Lulu's not so bad, you know," Trevor said. "If you're done with her, I'm more than happy to step in."

"I'm done. Trina is gonna keep me happy from now on."

She waved, scrunched up her nose and blew Sammy a kiss.

"I wanted to dump Lulu a while ago," he told Trevor. "When she first started getting too attached. I like 'em a little faster and a little meaner, if you catch my drift."

"Yeah, I catch it." Trevor looked Trina over good. Mean wasn't the first word that came to his mind. "I think I'll keep that date then. Li'l Lulu could probably use some consoling about now."

Sammy snickered, and Trevor took the wad of cash from Sammy's hand. Both lefties, they shook a hard goodbye.

"Next time you need a second, give me a ring. You're good on your word, and I could use the dough."

"Maybe. Something is coming up in Puerto Rico, around Christmas time. A horse race needs boosting. My connections back east say it'll involve swapping out horses. Big purse involved. It's too early for details, but I'll keep your number."

"Do that."

Trevor stuffed the cash inside his trench and made his way outside. Humming Zeppelin's "Stairway to Heaven," he thought of Lulu and ambled toward El Compadre. It was typical L.A. weather, seventy-something, and he walked to keep himself primed for later. He figured on getting lucky at the Lucky Lickety-Split tonight.

Back at the motel, Lulu walked to the mirror. She re-touched her mascara, smeared now from crying. She lifted her chin, grabbed her fake leopard print bag from the bed, and clicked her scuffed up heels across the dusty, wooden floor. The plastic eyes of Felix the Cat slid back and forth and the ants marched in time, as Lulu pushed out under a smoke-colored Los Angeles sky.

CAT WALKS INTO A BANK
Gobind Tanaka

"You okay?" Her stare continues to ask the question. "Looks like you saw a ghost."

Not sure how long I've been watching her spin a neon gel pen across her fingers. I was caught in a flashback of Lance Corporal Kim Johnson spinning a government-issued ballpoint. By itself a happy memory, but another always follows that chills me to the bone.

"I was just remembering something. Someone."

"I like your watch, by the way. Even though it's a man's watch."

I notice her wristwatch is small and ornate. Mine reads eleven hundred hours, 11:00 a.m. civilian time. "I just think of it as a regular watch. Tough to read hands on a little jewelry piece. Why should we have to strain our eyes more than men?"

I stretch my neck and roll my shoulders. Clear my head with a shake.

She smiles and looks me up and down, at least what she can see over the elevated bank deposit slip counter. Still unconsciously spinning her pen. "Your futuristic jacket is awesome, form fitting and stylish, yeah. But in this heat?"

"Armored motorcycle jacket, protects my spine and joints." I lift my helmet and skinny backpack into view above the counter. "Feels fine in the wind."

"Nice."

We stare at each other across the elevated counter, both holding down deposit slips. I'm starting to feel warm. I realize I'm blushing. I never blush.

I break the gaze and glance around the marble-floored bank. Very high ceiling. Parking lot access and a hallway at one end, a vault at the other. Loan officers at rows of desks. Half their customers Asian, the other half Hispanic or European. Asian Americans comprise a majority of Diamond Bar residents.

A middle-aged woman holds the front door from the street for a younger woman pushing a stroller, baby asleep.

Kim Johnson wanted to raise kids. I got to know all my Marines—their families, dreams. She taught kids, worked as an assistant teacher before enlisting. She planned to get her credential using G.I. Bill college benefits.

I tear up the deposit slip and stuff it in the counter's stupid little brass trash door.

The woman across from me laughs. "Yeah, I hate pushing paper into those tiny things too. You'd think it's the nineteenth century. Can't they just provide wastepaper baskets?"

I think I'm agreeing, but my voice comes out like a grunt. I'm still seeing Kim Johnson's face.

She wrinkles her forehead and frowns. "You really seem upset."

I clear my throat, set down the chained bank pen I've been holding, and sigh. Through the front window I watch the outside air shimmer, already in the nineties. I was glad to walk into air-conditioned comfort, but now I feel clammy and cold. Again. The bank A/C scrubs all odors, unlike my gunpowder- and blood-scented flashback.

"I sort of did see a ghost."

She raises her hands, palms facing me. "Hey, didn't mean that literally."

"I do. Well, not a ghost exactly." *Whoa. I almost confided in this complete stranger.*

I take a real look at her. She looks about thirty, like me. Athletic like me, but thinner, like a dancer. Narrow aristocratic face, Korean or Japanese. Nicely proportioned features, alert intelligent eyes. Not conventionally pretty by either American or Asian pop media standards, but lovely nonetheless.

I offer my hand. "Catherine Suzuki. Call me Cat." We shake.

"Traci Kim. Call me Kim. All my friends do." She grins. "I know, I know, like a million other 'Kims' in L.A. So who were you thinking of?"

"A, uh, a friend who died."

Her eyes fill with compassion. Empathy. "I'm so sorry. What happened? How did he die?"

"She. Combat. In a bank, actually." I grimace. "My squad stopped Iraqi bandits from robbing a bank in Kirkuk. A lance corporal took multiple rounds in the gut, armor-piercing. I took off her flak jacket, held her intestines. She lost too much blood."

"The shots missed you?"

"Most. I took a few in my vest, two in a leg."

"You were lucky."

I feel like she just punched me in the gut. "Lucky? I hate that word. Near the end of my tour I felt like I was on borrowed time. I lived. She died. So did all the robbers. Body count in our favor, battle success for The Brass, but we didn't care about that. We lost a comrade."

Kim looks contrite. I'm still pissed, but I know she doesn't deserve my anger. We stand silent, still.

The young mother with stroller stops at our counter, leans past me, and snags a deposit slip. She shares a sheepish smile with us and says, "Sorry."

Kim and I simultaneously say, "No problem."

I hear a *plop* and look down. A pacifier rolls to a stop on the floor. I squat, pull a napkin from a pocket, wipe the pacifier and hand it to the mother.

She smiles and says, "*Salamat po.*"

I reflexively respond, "*Walang anuman po.*"

The mother rolls the stroller over to a couple of chairs near a large-leafed potted plant. She calls the older woman *Tiya*, meaning Auntie. As the two women converse with a security guard, I soak in the soothing sing-song of Tagalog, familiar from childhood years spent playing at my Filipina friends' houses.

Kim and I look at each other again.

Kim says, "You survived." She pauses, nods to herself. "Survivor's guilt."

"Yeah. Big time. I was her squad leader, her sergeant. Why her? Why not me?"

We stare at each other a while. Kim glances around, as if noticing other people in the bank for the first time.

I shake my head. "I don't know why I told you that. Any of it. I never talk about it." *Why am I opening up to this person? I haven't shared this with doctors or other vets. Who wants to hear this anyway?*

Kim puts a hand to her heart. "Been happening my whole life. One night in Culver City a *Nisei* mechanic came over from his service bays to unlock his friend's tennis store. I'd been literally window shopping. While I test swung rackets, we chatted away. Eventually the mechanic talked about his time in the U.S. Army. Enemy fire wounded him in the Korean War. He heard a priest administer last rites over him in a MASH unit.

"'I couldn't move, couldn't speak,' he told me, 'just heard them say I wouldn't last until dawn.'

"That night he watched a yellow glow the size of a golf ball fly lazy figure-eights above him in the tent, occasionally swooping down to take him into the White Light.

"He told me, 'Each time I chased it off, saying I wasn't ready. In my mind I waved my arms, but I was in a coma. Then I opened my eyes, and all the doctors were surprised.'"

Kim points at me. "He told me, 'I don't know why I'm telling you this. I never told anyone, not even my wife.'" Kim shakes her head. "Used to think everyone heard private stories. Found out darn few people actually listen."

So she's a Trauma Whisperer. That's my name for people who do this. I've met several, and I've seen people confide in my father and sister. Always in a mundane social setting: grocery store, coffee shop—normal places.

First time I've been on the sharing side. Well, other than shrink appointments and group sessions at VA hospitals. In World War I they called it shellshock. In World War II and Korea they called it battle fatigue. Since the American War in Vietnam we call it post-traumatic stress syndrome, PTSD. It changes you.

Kim glances at the teller line. "You on a break, early lunch?"

"No, visiting my cousin. Running errands and killing time until she's free later."

"What's your line of work?"

"I'm figuring that out. Still new to civilian life, less than a year now. How about you?"

"I settle insurance claims, do investigations. Just conducted an interview near here. I'll get a business card from my purse. Do you have a card?"

"Negative. Well, I have my Marine Corps business card." I root in my cargo pants pocket for my card and she digs in her purse.

I watch an open teller number flash on the availability screen. I look back to our counter. Kim piles up stuff from her smooth leather shoulder bag: pens, receipts, small makeup case, flashlight. Inside her purse I glimpse panties, socks, some female necessities. A couple more items join the pile.

"Is that a selfie stick?"

"Yep." Kim stretches its telescoping shaft to about twenty inches and unfolds the phone holder. "Better photos with this."

"Hmm." Photos I take with my phone in outstretched hand shrink everything except my face. *Maybe I should get a stick.*

I make a crew of four as they enter, two from the front, two from the parking lot. They are self-assured, arrogant even.

Just like the crew that marched into that bank in Kirkuk, only to get surrounded by my MP squad because, well, we were there.

I take a deep breath. *Only a memory. Just a flashback.*

This quartet sports matching prism-hued mirror sunglasses and various pattern Hawaiian shirts in riotous colors instead of riot gear or cheap criminal togs. Besides L.A.'s thriving community of real Hawaiians, only musicians, hipsters, and class clowns wear Hawaiian shirts.

In my mind musicians can wear whatever they want—it's the sound that counts—and I do see them all over L.A. wearing "whatever." But hipsters and clowns are lame. I would dismiss these four dudes as harmless dorks but for the long cylindrical duffel each carries slung cross-body to keep hands free. The duffels sag from weight.

Maybe it's sports equipment. They're jocks.

All four start texting on their phones.

Kim finds her business card, puts the pile back into her purse. She hands me her card, reads mine. "*Captain* Suzuki. United States Marine Corps Military Police. Like NCIS?"

"No, NCIS agents are civilians, and they investigate. MPs police."

"So-o, like shore patrol?"

"No, shore patrol is just a duty assigned to any sailor—they just put on an SP armband. USMC Military Police is an MOS."

She looks puzzled.

"Sorry. MOS means military occupational specialty. It's a numeric code for a job. As MPs we guard things, basically. Ships, embassies, bases. Brass if called upon. That's the short version." *No need to get into gory details. Yet I already have.*

Kim purses her lips, shakes her head. "Brass what?"

"Big brass. Comes from insignia." I tap where a general pins his collar star, then the crest of my shoulder, where his epaulet would hold another. "High ranking officers, VIPs, that sort of thing."

"Oh. Wait, you were a sergeant and a captain?"

"Came through the ranks to become an officer. We call that a mustang."

"Cool." Kim looks at the baby in the stroller, checks out the length of the teller line. "Hey, I'm sorry for that choice of words before. Of course you weren't lucky, you lost a friend."

The word "friend" jars me, even though I used it first. I pivot a bit, enough to scan the lobby again. Checking out my environment is a habit I deliberately keep sharp, but at this moment I just turn away and clamp down my jaw. *I will NOT tear up.*

Lance Corporal Kim Johnson's life was my responsibility— as was her death. As sergeant and squad leader I carried responsibility for each Marine I commanded. Not friends. Marines. In some ways closer than family.

Kim gets my attention. "Hey, I gotta a transaction to make. This cell phone number current?"

"Affirmative."

"Want to get tea or coffee sometime?"

"Sure." I return her wave as she gets in line. I think she just asked me out on a date. Without setting a date. Like getting permission to ask me out.

Maybe. For sure. Hope flutters inside me.

Maybe. Doubt creeps in.

Can I let myself feel attraction, infatuation again? At eighteen I got clear on my sexuality, then served my enlisted and early Annapolis years under Don't Ask, Don't Tell. I kept people at a distance as an officer, easy to do as a Marine MP.

After years of service I came home. Got counseling. My family is fine with it, but I don't know many lesbians. I don't know many people period.

I got other counseling too, about combat, coming home. Talked with other vets. I started to regain a civilian perspective six months after I got back to The World. "In Country" means the combat zone while "The World" means home, civilian life. Gradually I got away from wondering every time a person passed me on the street if they packed a knife, gun, IED.

The real work came after that, dealing with the consequences of my combat actions, my experiences. It's true what they say; I remember every face. What I saw of the faces, anyway—before death, after, or both.

I look out the front window at immaculate storefronts across the boulevard. This kind of town accentuates my disconnection between war and peace. There is no war here, yet there is little calm, little satisfaction. People fuss over stuff we never think about at a base checkpoint, an embassy gate, standing watch on an aircraft carrier. Arguments over parking spaces or restaurant reservations. Complaints about slow traffic or the weather. Debating perceived flaws in perfectly fine products we can't even get in a war zone.

The four Hawaiian Shirts stand near the doors they came in. They aren't conducting any business like the customers around the bank, just staring at their phones. Not one sets down a heavy duffel.

I'm about dead center in the lobby, far from the parking exit. I might make it past these guys and out the front way if I walk now, might get to my bike in the lot. Or not, and I'm better off here for sight lines.

Besides, what if I'm wrong? Odds are slightly better for a flash mob. Lightning won't strike me twice, right?

I shift my stance to watch the entire crew via peripheral vision. Unstylish military haircuts, flat tops with buzz cut side-walls. A severe version of what we call "high and tight." All white guys, their looks ranging from Slavic to Black Irish to blond.

One of the things I like about spending time here—or any-where in The 626—is feeling normal, just a human being. Here folks don't come up and ask "What are you?" or tell me "Your English is very good." Here I'm not treated as a foreigner. My family has lived in California for five generations, since 1898.

I had to deal with some prejudice in The Corps. Some Vietnam, Korea, and WWII vets hate all Asians. Others travel to countries they fought in and visit former enemies, now com-rades, so I don't judge books by their covers. I'm complexion neutral.

Clothing though, I judge, because people express themselves in their presentation, or lack thereof. And even more by their focus, stance, actions. These Hawaiian Shirts are sketchy—they just don't belong.

Diamond Bar is right next to the 57 and 60 freeways. Partly because of its network of freeways, L.A. is the bank robbery capitol of the world.

I check my watch again. Freeways are parking lots during rush hour, but it's just after eleven, so the 57 and the 60 are wide-open.

I examine one hipster/clown, then another. Might have thin, lightweight Kevlar vests under those wild shirts. Or, maybe they're just 'roid ripped.

The Hawaiian Shirts simultaneously pocket their phones. They spread out to points that cover the entire lobby. All four nod to a tall woman with jet-black dyed hair in the teller line.

Jet-Black ducks under the vinyl band bordering the teller line. She drops a note on the branch manager's desk and pulls a long barrel .44 Magnum out of her gigantic tote bag.

Not just any .44 mag revolver, either. It looks like an actual Smith & Wesson Model 29 with six-and-a-half-inch barrel. *The effing Dirty Harry hand cannon.* Its powerful recoil will lift the barrel way above target after every shot, just like you see in the Clint Eastwood movies. Bad for shot grouping.

These observations and thoughts come from the part of me trained to coolly evaluate potential enemy combatants or criminals. As sergeant I would decide how to order my squad to deal with the threat. As captain I would deploy my company.

I lower my center of gravity below my navel and raise my mind and intuition to my third eye.

Another part of me resides at my heart, where I feel emotions I've worked hard to recover. I know the heart-in-my-throat feeling.

Jet-Black takes an isosceles stance. She looks stout enough to handle the pain of her gun's recoil, and holding the big weapon in the branch manager's face she certainly gets his attention. First step in getting his cooperation.

Folks at desks near the manager watch in stunned silence.

People in line are facing the opposite way, toward the tellers. Except for my new friend Kim. She's been watching her environment as if it were performance art, probably the only non-bored person in line. Her eyes bug out at the sight of Jet-Black drawn down on the manager.

A young redheaded customer with acne notices Kim staring. He follows her gaze and his eyes bug just like Kim's. "Omigod, omigod, omigod!" he shrieks. Seems like twenty times. Each iteration rises an octave until he squeaks.

Jet-Black nods to the Hawaiian Shirts. They unzip duffels and extract long guns: two shotguns and two AR-15s.

People gasp at the weapons, disbelieving. Most go quiet. A few shout in anger, or scream in fear, or babble. Their voices meld into a chorus of gibberish.

We can't predict how we will react to a dire situation. Not the first time, nor the tenth. Extensive conditioning enables military and law enforcement professionals to respond as trained—more or less. That gives them an edge, but even that is no guarantee.

I'm reacting for the first time in years with a civilian mindset, but I carry my combat training and experience. I've seen carnage from weapons like these, so I'm never surprised, exactly. I carry the trauma as well—it's always a shock.

Customers and bank officers turn in their chairs to look at the commotion and see the weapons display. A few officers reach under the lip of their desk; unseen fingers probably press silent alarm buttons. Other officers sit up as their jaws drop.

At the parking lot end of the lobby, one Hawaiian Shirt sports a fake-looking scar on his cheek. A prosthetic. Rifle at the ready, Scar approaches the security guard. "Hand over your weapon, carefully."

The guard is nonreactive, attentive and calm. Middle aged, but lean and hard. The way he flicks his gaze at the other gunmen makes me think he would take Scar one-on-one. Not his first rodeo. He unholsters his pistol and gives it to Scar.

The young Filipina mother covers the baby. Her *tiya* shields them both.

I face the tellers, pretending to watch Young Red freak, and pan my gaze to watch everything. Because I'm a lefty, I notice all the Hawaiian Shirts are righties. Each holds their weapon at an identical low ready position. *Trained by the same trainer.* Yet the way they stand and move says amateur. I find amateurs dangerous in their own unpredictable ways.

Customers huddle together or stand frozen, alone. A few get on their phones or even appear to take photos or video. The nice men with guns persuade them to give up their phones.

Scar orders the patrons in the teller area to lie down. Most collapse or dive to the floor. Young Red staggers about, screaming and squeaking, until Scar slams his rifle butt against Young Red's head.

Customers gasp and scream. Hawaiian Shirts stomp around yelling, "Shut up. Shut up." Customers quiet down.

I feel bad for Young Red, splayed out on the cold marble. I feel bad for everyone here. I think of my wounded and killed Marines, cut down too young. Lives changed, or ended. I brought home as many as I could.

I want these people to go home today. I look at Kim. I want her to survive.

I take a deep breath. *Be a Marine again.* I look around for a weapon. *That.* I snap a pen off its beaded metal chain and palm it. I scan the bank.

The branch manager leads Jet-Black into the vault. Watching them from the vault door, a sun-bleached blond with flattop like a bristle brush wields a shotgun. I designate him Bristle.

Bristle says to a customer, "Sit down. You aren't going anywhere unless I say so."

The Slavic-looking dude positions himself to cover the loan officers and applicants. He taps his shotgun muzzle on a desk, snaps his fingers several times for their attention. I designate him Snaps.

The Black Irish gunman pulls on his ear lobe. Repeatedly. I designate him Tic.

Tic tells the tellers, "Empty your drawers, and don't push any alarm buttons."

Horses are out of that barn, buddy.

Scar apparently thinks Kim is too slow to drop. He pushes her ahead of him away from the tellers. My eyes meet Kim's as they pass. I needn't have worried about Scar noticing my attention; he's focused on Kim's backside.

Oh-oh. Red flag.

I pocket the pen and follow as if ordered, but far enough behind that Scar doesn't notice. They turn into the hallway.

He pushes Kim into a cheaply furnished break room. I stop at the doorway. Scar backs Kim against the far wall and says, "Take off your clothes."

For sure I'm not letting this happen. I glide into the break room and pick up a broom leaning against a vending machine.

Kim keeps her eyes locked on Scar. *Good girl.* She crosses her arms and juts out her chin. "So you aren't a professional bank robber. You're just an asshole."

Scar holds up his rifle. "I'm an asshole with a gun. See?"

Holding the broom handle like a rifle with attached bayonet, I thrust its tip into Scar's head just above his neck. Scar stumbles in place, out cold on his feet. I leap up, reach over the top of his head to claw at his forehead, and chop a knife hand blow to his throat.

Scar falls to the white marble floor. Even if he comes to, he won't be talking soon.

"Kim," I whisper. "Help me get him out of sight."

We drag Scar into a janitorial closet. I find zip ties on a bottom shelf and hogtie his wrists to his ankles. Back in the break room, I point at a table. "Okay, Kim, you sit there. Face the closet with your hands up like he's covering you."

Kim nods. She stares wide-eyed at Scar bound on the floor.

Listening for any approach, I pick up Scar's AR-15. I move the safety switch to the safe position—with great care. A buddy accidentally discharged an unfamiliar rifle by flipping a badly designed safety switch too far, so I'm careful with any strange gun.

I drop the magazine and find it full. I rack the slide to ensure no round is in the barrel. I shake the rifle; the sling swivels rattle. I find duct tape, DIY best friend, and silence the swivels. I slap in the mag, rack again to put one in the pipe.

Good to go. I flip the safety down to the fire position. I'm glad these are true civilian weapons. Full automatic fire is imprecise, best used for suppression. Here in the bank, full auto bursts could wound a lot of people.

I push the door away from the wall a bit to hide behind, but I also position myself beyond the swing so it won't smash my face or weapon. I stand in high ready position.

Kim gives me a look.

I respect her skepticism, but I say only, "It'll be okay."

A man's deep voice booms out in the hall. "Dude, we don't have time for your crap."

Kim raises her hands.

Tic enters the break room, sees Kim. "What are you doing? Where's…that guy?" He almost says a name.

Kim remains silent, stares at the closet. Tic keeps talking, advancing toward Kim. He pauses to pull on his ear.

I step out behind him and clock him with the rifle butt. Tic face plants on white marble.

Kim and I drag him into the closet and lay him beside Scar.

I unload Tic's ammo into my cargo pockets, hide his rifle inside a low cabinet against the opposite wall, and we reset. I can tell by the way she fidgets that Kim is having a hard time with the adrenaline surge.

Snaps cautiously enters the break room. I see his face react when he catches a glimpse of me through the gap at the door hinges. As he swings his shotgun around I step out firing the AR-15. My first round whizzes over his shoulder. The next two hit his torso, center mass.

The sound of Snaps's shotgun blast echoes off the hard floor and walls, ringing in my ears. His buckshot hits the marble and several pellets bounce up into my shins.

I ignore the pain and shoot him through the cheek. *No flak jacket up there.*

Brain matter flies out the back of his skull and his breath shudders.

I step over the corpse and stick my head out into the hall. Bristle is coming with his shotgun. I pull back, my pulse banging in my head.

Bristle's shotgun fills the hall with heat and buckshot. My

ears begin to hear again—customers are screaming with each gunshot.

I pop out and send three shots in return.

Bristle ducks behind a corner.

I pull back into the break room as his next blast flies by.

Trapped. Have to stay ready to hit Bristle if he rushes me, hold out for the cavalry. I glance around quickly.

"What are you looking for?" Kim stays crouched behind a chair.

"You got anything in that huge bag of tricks I can use as an extendable mirror?"

Kim fumbles in her purse, attaches a compact mirror to her selfie stick. "Here."

"Wow, cool."

We tilt a table onto the floor and I return to the doorway with the mirror.

Kim gets behind the table and peeks over. "You're bleeding."

"Uh, gee, thanks for the reminder." I feel the hot metal now, each ball of buckshot searing its own hole into a shinbone.

I flip down the light switch to darken the break room. I ease Kim's mirror just out the doorway near the floor, steady as I can so it doesn't grab Bristle's attention. To see him in the mirror I have to face away from him, so I plan out where to place my feet to spin and shoot.

Empty corridor. He could be staying around either corner where the hall spills into the lobby.

Faraway sirens get louder. Cops should be here soon, to surround and communicate, or maybe just crash.

A small caliber handgun fires. Jet-Black's .44 Magnum booms. More shouts and screams. In the mirror, Bristle's blond head and flower shirt bob away.

I set down the mirror, spin into the hall. My feet slide on buckshot as I sprint to the lobby.

Near the vault, the guard holds a small hideout pistol—a standoff with Jet-Black holding a vault bag of loot in one hand.

Twenty yards from them, Bristle fires a round and his buckshot sprays the guard and some customers. Jet-Black fires away at the falling guard.

As I draw a bead on Bristle's head, the now prone guard returns fire, hitting Bristle's body armor. The low-caliber bullets let Bristle to stay on his feet, but make him stagger out of my sight picture. I align my iron sight on his head again and squeeze twice.

Bristle goes down.

Jet-Black fires a wild shot past me, swings back to the guard as he rolls up to a half kneeling position. The guard's next shot clips her ear and her shades break into flying fragments. She grunts, drops her vault bag to use a two-handed grip and shoots the guard in the shoulder.

I put my front sight on her reddening ear. Customers and staff fill the bottom of my sight picture, a shooting term for what I see around my front sight. *Got to take the shot.* I drop one knee to the floor, elevating my shot angle enough toward the ceiling to miss innocents.

I hope.

I squeeze the trigger.

Jet-Black, her exposed eyes manic, blinks in the light. She swings her arms around to bear on me.

Front sight, front sight. Forcing myself to be gentle, I squeeze again.

"Felix. You need to hold this." I shove the AR-15 beneath the guard's arm resting on the floor.

"Huh?" The guard is lucid, we've been talking as I staunched his bleeding, but he doesn't know why I'm talking about the rifle.

"I can't be holding weapons when the cops enter. They'll shoot me for sure."

"The robbers are all down."

"I don't want the *cops* to shoot me." My voice shakes a bit. I force myself to breathe.

"Right. Disarmed. Good idea." Felix grimaces in pain.

I fold my jacket under Felix's head for a pillow. I apply pressure to the gauze pad I hold on his entry wound and re-check the gauze on his exit wound.

"Besides," I say, "there's the Vietnam vet thing. I had to deal with old Marines sometimes, and not all of them loved Vietnamese people."

Felix focuses on me. Sparks fly from his gaze. "Loved? They hated Vietnamese. Everyone they shot was Vietnamese. Everyone who shot *at* them was Vietnamese. They saw all ARVN as unreliable, no matter how many competent soldiers fought alongside. They saw all civilians as hidden Viet Cong, no matter how many they met."

I change the dressing on Felix's shoulder. "You were there?"

"No, I was Philippine Marines—busy fighting Moros. But lots of veterans told me how they felt. And other guys told me how in basic training and boot camp they got stood up front. Trainers and D.I.s pointed at their faces and said, 'This is what the enemy looks like.' Called them every vile name they learned In Country. That continued for years after the last U.S. troops pulled out."

I go very still. I've been called some of those names.

Felix mumbles something in rough Tagalog, including expletives. He glares again. "They came home and saw all Asians as the enemy."

A bullhorn at the front door: "This is the Los Angeles County Sheriff's Department. We are entering the bank. Put your hands on your head and stay perfectly still."

I sit on my heels next to Felix, face the front door and put my hands on my head.

"Hey, don't worry, Cat, all Vietnam vets retired now. Veterans who are cops now, they want to shoot Arabs, Afghans, Pakistanis. Sikhs because they wear turbans. They don't shoot us. We don't look like Omar Sharif."

"Who?"

Felix rolls his eyes and drops his head on my jacket. "You're too young."

A dozen deputies swarm in, sweeping their eyes and weapons across everyone in the bank. White, black, Hispanic—and Asian. I believed Felix, but only now do I breathe easy.

Each cop starts to check every person. Once cleared, people keep their hands on head and move toward the front door.

Kim rushes out of the hallway. She carries the rifle and shotgun like a pair of fresh-caught salmon, grasping their muzzles like gills. "There are more robbers back there."

A bunch of guns point her way. My heart stops a moment. "Customer!" I yell. "She's a customer!"

Déjà vu.

A big male voice calls out, "Put the weapons down! Now!"

Kim yells out, "Don't shoot!" She drops the guns and points back toward the break room. The guns hit the floor, bounce and flip into the air like giant dancing sticks of dynamite.

I hold my breath until the guns stop bouncing.

The attempted robbery felt like hours, but the entire incident lasted only twenty minutes. With a sheriff's station right in Diamond Bar, the first few LASD deputies arrived within ten minutes of the alarms. They barely had time to cordon off the street before all the shooting. Took a lot longer for the deputies to sort out these witnesses and conduct preliminary interviews.

The first team of paramedics does triage. Since I'm walking, they'll deal with me after the guard and customers suffering from worse wounds. More paramedics arrive to put those folks on gurneys and rush them to the hospital.

Kim and I comfort each other with a hug. Kim looks down at Jet-Black, collapsed just a few feet away. "Is she alive?"

An EMT bandaging Jet-Black looks up at us. Her nametag patch reads CHEN. "Knocked out. The bullet bounced off her skull. Amazing it didn't penetrate."

I shake my head. "She's hard headed."

EMT Chen moves off to patch a wound on a nearby bank customer.

I feel the pen in my pocket and pull it out. I dangle its broken chain like a lizard's stumpy tail.

Kim looks at the pen. "What's that doing in your pocket?"

I chuckle. "Took it off the counter. Weapon of last resort; glad I didn't need it. Guess they'll charge me for it. Hey, hope they don't call it theft."

Kim cackles. "That would make you a bank robber." We laugh together, louder than the joke deserves, but it feels so good. What a relief.

EMT Chen returns to Jet-Black, says to her partner, "Thready pulse. Shooting one CC of epinephrine to keep her from going into shock." She thumps Jet-Black's vein by flicking a fingertip. She slides a syringe needle in, and pushes the plunger. She sets aside the syringe and lifts Jet-Black's eyelid, checks pulse again on the throat. "Should respond soon. When do we get a gurney here?"

Jet-Black abruptly sits up like a puppet on a string and knocks aside Chen's hands. Jet-Black blinks her eyes several times. The EMTs, Kim, and I all stare. I look around—deputies working all over the bank, all busy.

I turn back to see Jet-Black palm strike Chen to the face. She sees me and says, "You!" She pulls off her belt buckle to wield a push knife between fisted fingers, a two-inch double-edged blade. She crawls and lunges out from her knees.

I sweep Kim to the side. Jet-Black thrusts the knife at me.

I pivot off-line and parry. I bring my pen hand up and over Jet-Black's arm, thrust the pen into her throat, then tackle her facedown to the floor.

She twists her wrist to slash at me. A hardhead indeed.

I pound hammer fists on a pressure point near the crook of her elbow, numbing her fingers. I grab her knife and toss it to the floor.

I get one of her arms into a surfboard wrestling hold and press my bodyweight on her upper back. Jet-Black tries to roll, but I counter. She pulls the pen out of her throat and blood gushes as she tries to stab me. Applying a wristlock I disarm her. Jet-Black bucks under me a few times more and goes still.

Holding her bruised cheek EMT Chen cautiously approaches us. She checks Jet-Black's pulse, drops her shoulders. She looks at me and shakes her head. Only then do I sit up.

Chen says, "You okay?"

Am I okay?

Yes.

No.

Maybe.

Weak-kneed and exhausted, Kim and I limp out of the bank. We hunker down on a concrete bench near the parking lot. The team that worked on Jet-Black finds us and finishes triage. After pronouncing Kim intact, Chen treats my buckshot wounds.

Chen's male partner says, "No running for a while. Once you get home keep your feet elevated."

Chen holds up a small plastic jar. Inside: bloody buckshot pellets that had been lodged in my legs. "I would give you a souvenir, but this is crime scene evidence."

We also see white shards she extracted. Kim says, "What are those white things?"

Chen gives a wry grin. "Slivers of the bank floor."

Bank floor. Reminds me. "Hey, how is the bank guard?"

"Felix. Tough dude. He lost some blood, but your first aid helped. The buckshot stopped shallow, the bullet went through and through, missed bone. He should be fine if there are no complications. He's in top shape, especially for his age."

"How old is he?"

"Sixty."

"Wow. I thought he was forty, forty-five. Another baby-faced Asian."

We chuckle. Chen says, "Yeah, we'll be happy about that when we're older. But Felix is really fit. You know, I think he could outrun both of us."

I grin. "Or outfight us."

"Well, that's your department." Chen taps my eagle, globe, and anchor tattoo, visible between buckshot bandages. "I see where you got your training. My uncle was in The Corps. By the way, wasn't this tattoo painful to get on your shin?"

"Not as painful as this buckshot."

Detectives arrive to take statements. As I answer their questions I start to shake, especially my knees. My body always does this after action. Especially in debrief when, like now, I talk about it and let myself think how things could have gone way worse. Like in that bank in Kirkuk.

Satisfaction is a relative thing. Three new faces flash in to haunt my mind's eye. Snaps. Bristle. Jet-Black. Lifelong company. But the faces of Kim, Felix, and the rest of these folks won't be joining them.

Kim and I walk toward our vehicles, but we both stop in the parking lot. We face each other. We both jangle our keys.

Kim's face is flushed. She shuffles her feet.

My heart is beating fast again, my mouth is dry, and I feel myself blushing. Again. I take a deep breath in and push it out. "Want to get that coffee right now?"

"Don't need any caffeine after this." She dismisses the bank with her hand, sees my disappointment, and grins. "How about lunch? I'm starving."

"Cool beans. You know any restaurants in DB?"

Kim chuckles. "No, I don't know places here either, but I bet we can find a lunch special nearby. Oh, too late for lunch."

I feel disappointed again.

Kim slides her arm inside mine and bumps shoulders. "Cheer up. We'll figure it out."

I do feel good. We stroll away from the cars, toward the street. "For sure. We can always get *boba*." I cover her hand with mine. "Or see a matinee. Just not an action movie, okay?"

THE END JUSTIFIES THE MEANS

Tony Chiarchiaro

I hated my boss; resented everything about her...her arrogance, her rudeness, the total lack of compassion toward her employees. I admit I was jealous. She had achieved so much in a relatively short span of time. And to boot, she hadn't even graduated from high school, yet she ordered me around like I was some dummy. After all, I was a college graduate. I had struggled to put myself through college, but somehow wound up working for a damned high school dropout.

Dorothy Halladay had taken the small company she had inherited, Gallery Metal Stamping, Inc., and built it into one of the most successful metal stamping businesses in Los Angeles County. She had done it essentially by shrewdness, by taking advantage of her employees, and by using any other unscrupulous means necessary to further her goals. Everybody knew her motto was "The end justifies the means."

"Arthur, I need to talk to you," she rattled off one day, in front of the whole management team. "Damn it, Arthur, production is way down. You're the general manager, I hold you responsible. If you can't get these employees to put out more,

I'll get somebody who can, *comprende?*" she said, her dark hair framing a face full of venom.

It wasn't just what she said, but how she said it. There was something about her that was vile, nasty, almost evil. Her shrill voice made my skin crawl. I hate to admit it, but she intimidated me.

Especially frustrating was that this humiliation was being delivered by a woman, when women were always supposed to be respectful to men in my culture. How could this be happening to me, a sophisticated, Mexican-American man?

"Sure, Dorothy," I said, "I...I'll try my best. We...we'll have a meeting today and I'll go over our production goals again. It's just that Sophia's been out sick. Her machine has been down."

"Well, then I guess that means the rest of the operators are just going to have to work that much harder, doesn't it?" she spat out, causing my stomach to churn.

Trembling with anger, I could feel the rage rising within me, the rush of adrenalin pounding through every fiber of my being. I felt like she had taken my pride and eviscerated it with her razor-sharp tongue.

That's when I realized it had to be done. I had to kill her. I didn't care what could happen as a consequence.

Once I made the decision, a sense of calm came over me.

It'll be easy. I know her daily routine. I'll make it look like a robbery gone bad. She always works late on Tuesday evenings. I could wait for her in the darkness of the parking garage while she goes to her car, the new Lexus SUV. (I drove a beat up old Toyota Corolla with a hundred and eighty-five thousand miles on it.)

I'd always disliked the parking garage. The huge concrete pillars, the grayness of it all. Now it was perfectly appropriate...so accommodating. The massive cement walls and support columns created lots of shadowy areas where one could hide...and wait.

On the following Tuesday night, I made my way to the parking structure and secreted myself near her Lexus. I had purchased a long butcher knife from the local swap meet using cash so it couldn't be traced. I wore rubber gloves so fingerprints wouldn't be an issue. I'd covered all the bases.

Alone in the dimly lit structure at eight o'clock sharp, I waited patiently. At eight-fifteen, the last car, other than Dorothy's, left the location. I crouched down low in the darkness so nobody could see me. It was perfect.

At eight-twenty-five, I heard the clickety-clack of her high heels and saw her approach the Lexus parked only ten feet away from my place of concealment. When I recognized the jingle of her keys and the sound of the car door opening I made my move. Like a predator pouncing upon an unwary prey, there was never a question of whether I would do it or not. I was actually surprised by my boldness.

Eight-inch blade in hand, it was my intention to grab her from behind and thrust the sharpened knife into her back, just below the rib cage, then upward into her heart. But somehow, she must have sensed my presence. At the last second, she turned around and faced me, letting out a gasp. I had no choice but to look into her eyes as I thrust the steel blade deep into her midsection. She managed to blurt out, "Arthur... what are you...doing? Are you crazy?"

"I'll show you how crazy I am," I answered as she fell backward against the driver's seat of the Lexus. I continued to thrust the knife again and again under her rib cage and into her heart, that cold, cold heart, until her initial cry became a whimper; until her body was limp and lifeless.

Looking through her prescription glasses into her eyes, I saw her stare out into space. Her hateful eyes, dull, lifeless. Even in death, she still seemed to mock me, her mouth contorted in a kind of sneering expression...still reflecting disdain. Damn, I detested her.

"You won't hurt my feelings anymore. You won't hurt anybody's feelings anymore," I spat out at her, saliva spraying her hateful face. The face that caused so much pain to so many.

I rifled through her purse to create the illusion of a robbery. I placed her lifeless body prone on the concrete floor in the empty space adjacent to her car, facedown resting on an oil stain.

Removing eighty dollars in cash from her purse, I tossed the empty bag along with the rest of its contents into a trash container about a hundred feet away. I deposited the knife there, too.

At home later that evening, I sat back and reflected upon what I had accomplished. No remorse. Dorothy Halladay would bring no more sorrow to anyone. I felt as though I'd committed the perfect crime, and that the world had been relieved of a real burden.

Several months went by uneventfully. Work was much less stressful. The business had been taken over by Dorothy's nephew, Edward Borischolski, who was a people-oriented manager. Employee morale was up and so was production. I was proud of the turnaround from what I attributed to my own courageous activity.

That's why I was completely surprised when I answered my door one evening and saw two uniformed deputies and several detectives waiting there.

"Are you Arthur W. Martinez?" the officer closest to me asked.

I nodded my head ever so slightly. "Maybe. Who are you?"

"Mr. Martinez, I'm Detective Bell and this is Detective Chopak. We're here to place you under arrest for the murder of Dorothy Halladay."

I felt my mouth drop. I sensed my freedom evaporating like so many clouds on a windy day. After listening to the detective recite my Miranda rights, I asked in a slightly arrogant tone,

"On what basis are you making these outrageous accusations?"

"Well, Mr. Martinez, you know we live in a highly technical society these days. Our forensic analysis has evolved over the years in keeping with the advances in technology.

"To make a long story short, in the course of our investigation, we discovered there were some spots on the victim's glasses. Based upon an educated guess, we hypothesized that the spots may have come from the killer who we concluded was facing the victim as he murdered her. We carefully examined the spots, removed the glasses for safekeeping under very precise guidelines for evidence gathering and storage. Once that was done, we began our interviews with each and every employee of Gallery Metal Stamping, among others.

"As you may recall, it was a very hot day when you had your interview at our headquarters. We offered, and you accepted a can of Coca Cola. We in fact offered cans of Coke or other soft drinks to all of our potential suspects. If they declined the drink, we obtained subpoenas and court orders for samples of their saliva. In your case that wasn't necessary. From the can of Coke you drank, we obtained your saliva sample.

"We had the spots from Ms. Halladay's glasses analyzed in our laboratory and confirmed the spots were saliva. So, we next compared the DNA gathered from the saliva collected from Ms. Halladay's glasses to that which was obtained from the Coke can from which you drank.

"And, lo and behold, there was a perfect match with the DNA from the can, to the DNA gathered from the saliva sprayed upon Ms. Halladay's glasses during the course of her murder.

"You erred, Mr. Martinez, when you somehow managed to get your spit all over the deceased's face and prescription glasses. Thus, I repeat, Mr. Martinez, the DNA match between the saliva found on Ms. Halladay and upon her glasses is exactly the same as yours. In conclusion, you are the killer, Mr. Martinez."

After contemplating the detective's statement for a fleeting moment, I realized that my life as I knew it was over, and that the possibility of the death penalty was very real. Yet, I couldn't restrain myself.

"You know what, Detective, I hated that woman. I'd do it all over again, and if you would have known her the way I knew her, maybe you'd understand. She had to go. Oh, yeah, she had to go...anyway, anyhow. Like she used to say, 'The end justifies the means.'"

SHIFTING REFLECTIONS
Julie G. Beers

"Cut it off."

"Are you sure?" Fiona was hesitant.

Kelly nodded. "I need to be free of her."

Snip. Snip. Snip. With each cut, Kelly felt lighter, freer. The long dark curls fell to the floor, creating a huge pile. A shampoo girl swept the hair up then disappeared into the back of the crowded West Hollywood salon.

Fiona raised her scissors. "Are you sure you're ready for this? It's a drastic change."

"I'm sure," Kelly ran her hands through the newly cut hair. "I love it already."

Fiona smiled, "I always say that a new style can change your life."

"That's what I'm hoping for. It's time to shake things up... live a little. I've been living in the past for too long."

Fiona patted Kelly's shoulder sympathetically. "Any news about your sister?"

Kelly shook her head. "It's as if Jill stepped off the edge of the earth." Her eyes suddenly teared up and Fiona handed her a tissue. "I thought that maybe she went on a vacation or something, but..." Kelly paused for a long moment. "I've got to admit to myself that Jill is a hopeless cause. It's the drugs. It's always been the drugs."

"From what you've told me, it's hard to believe she's your twin," Fiona murmured.

"We may be twins but we've always been complete opposites, even before we were born. My mother swore we fought each other in the womb."

"The good twin and the evil one."

"Not evil. No matter how bad it got, I'll never say that about Jill. But she was always so irresponsible that I felt I had to be the opposite. I suppose I've been a bit obsessed with building a secure future."

"There's nothing wrong with that," stated Fiona.

"I wish my sister felt that way. Our parents left us each a sizeable sum. I invested my inheritance carefully and it paid off."

"What about your sister? Is she rich, too?"

"Not anymore. Jill went through her money quickly and then she asked me to buy out her share of our parents' home. I did, of course. On the condition that she enter rehab—which I also paid for."

Fiona nodded, "You were really there for her."

"Stupidly, I thought I could save her. Rehab after rehab. I thought the last one worked, but…"

"Sounds like she's not ready to change," Fiona declared as she set the scissors aside.

Kelly nodded. "I've been stuck in the rut of cleaning up Jill's messes my whole life. Our last fight before she took off was…brutal." Kelly wiped away another tear. "That's why I bought the condo on the Westside. Just too many memories in the Los Feliz house."

"I completely understand." The hairdresser turned to mix Kelly's color.

"I pray that my sister's okay, but if I'm being honest—"

"You want her to stay out of your life."

"Exactly. I'm learning that we can't change others, we can only change ourselves."

"Too true," agreed Fiona.

"But every time I look in the mirror, I'm haunted by her."

"Well, I can take care of that," grinned Fiona. She began to apply the color to Kelly's short hair. "Let's look to the future. *Your* future. And a whole new makeover."

"Thanks for being so understanding, Fi. I'm so happy that I moved here and discovered you."

"My pleasure." Fiona eyed her client in the mirror. "Let's turn you into a rock star."

A couple of hours later, Kelly, rocking a blonde pixie, was all smiles as she left the salon. She decided it was time to get the wardrobe to match the new hair and headed for the Beverly Center. She was surprised to find a parking space so easily. Things were changing for the better every second.

Inside the mall, the sparkles of a jewelry store immediately caught her attention. She studied the effervescent assortment and asked to see several pieces. As she tried on a stunning diamond tennis bracelet, a familiar face and cascade of brown curls reflected in the mirror backing the counter. Kelly spun around, but her sister wasn't there. She raced to the store's entrance and scanned the crowd.

A strong hand clamped on her shoulder. "Miss, are you planning on purchasing that bracelet?" The burly security guard was polite but he meant business.

Kelly nodded. "Of course. I'm so sorry, I just thought I saw someone..." She looked toward the crowd again. "But it can't be."

The guard firmly steered her back into the store before re-leasing his grip. Kelly knew he thought she was going to steal the jewelry and it irked her. She didn't need to steal anything. She was rich. Returning to the counter, Kelly smiled at the sales clerk. "Let's see how much damage I can do with my credit card today."

She returned home to her penthouse condo with two diamond bracelets, a pair of earrings, a stunning leather jacket, and a week's worth of new clothes. The sleek condo was a sharp contrast to the old-world elegance of the Los Feliz mansion. Even though she'd barely started to furnish it, Kelly loved this place in the heart of the Sunset Strip action, so near to Beverly Hills and only a short drive from the beach. She dropped her purchases on the counter, poured a glass of pinot grigio, and stood on her balcony to watch the hazy California sun slowly set. She ran her hands through her newly shorn hair and smiled. Cutting ties to the past felt good. She felt free.

As dusk settled, she returned inside for more wine and noticed that a packing box in the corner had fallen over, partially spilling its contents on the floor. She hadn't brought much from the house—couldn't the movers have stacked things better? As Kelly approached the box, her glass slipped from her fingers and shattered on the marble tile. A photo album had fallen from the box and lay open to a childhood picture of Kelly and her twin sister. Identical dark curls blew in the wind as the twins rode their bikes in the mountains.

She didn't remember packing the photo album. Why would she bring it here? She slammed the album shut, shoved it back into the box, and then poured another glass of wine. The maid could sweep up the mess in the morning.

For the next few days, Kelly couldn't shake the feeling she was being watched. Several times she was sure she glimpsed the reflection of her sister in store windows. But, of course, her sister was never there. One afternoon, when she entered her car to drive to the salon for a manicure appointment, Kelly smelled her sister's favorite perfume, Opium. The scent was almost imperceptible, but there.

Kelly's hands shook a bit as she sat down for her manicure with Amber. Fiona rushed over to greet her, "I love your new outfit, and those shoes—" The stylist stopped short. "Are you okay? You look really pale."

"I think I'm being haunted." Kelly couldn't stop herself from blurting it out.

"Really?" Amber, the manicurist, paused.

Fiona sat down next to Kelly. "It's your sister, isn't it? I've heard about that twin sense thing."

"I don't know about that but..." Kelly took a deep breath and continued, "At first I thought I was being watched, but strange things have been happening all week. I know it's my sister and—"

"You think she's dead," Fiona interrupted. It was a statement, not a question.

Kelly nodded slowly. "It does seem otherworldly. I see her reflection everywhere. But no one is ever there."

Amber's eyes widened. "That's spooky."

Fiona seemed excited. "I've heard that ghosts appear in mirror images."

"Other strange things have been happening, too. Photos of the two of us show up in unexpected places. And when I got in my car to come here, I could swear I smelled my sister's perfume."

"She's trying to contact you," Fiona declared. "Twins have that strong connection, no matter how fractured it might seem." She grabbed Kelly's hands. "I know someone who can help. Have you heard of the psychic Gabriel Griggs?"

Kelly shook her head.

"He's a new client of mine. I was thrilled when Gabriel sought me out, and not just because he's a talented psychic. He's also gorgeous." Fiona turned to include Amber. "I've never seen Amber move that quickly to offer a manicure."

Amber grinned. "Gabriel's so handsome. And generous. He gave me a free reading as part of my tip. And let me tell you, he's for real. He knew things about me that, well, only a psychic could possibly know."

"I'm not sure I believe in all that psychic stuff."

"Did you believe in hauntings before this?" asked Fiona.

"I guess not...But I don't think it's a good idea to aggravate the situation. It might make things worse."

"Nonsense," argued Fiona. "The situation is already worse. You need help and, trust me, Gabriel's the guy."

"I'm sure he can help you," agreed Amber.

"I'm calling him right now." Fiona moved to the phone.

Gabriel Griggs arrived an hour later, and Fiona introduced him to Kelly. The tall, dark-haired psychic was every bit as handsome as Amber had promised. His brown eyes radiated warmth and concern as he took Kelly's hand.

"Fiona told me about your situation." Gabriel continued to hold her hand, and Kelly felt an immediate attraction.

"I feel a bit silly," she stammered. "Maybe I'm overreacting. I mean my sister could be fine. I don't know; maybe she's hurt. Maybe she's...I don't know why I'm babbling."

Well, that wasn't quite true. She did know why. She always babbled when she was nervous about making a good impression.

"Don't feel silly." He gently caressed Kelly's hand, which made her tingle. "You want to know what's going on, and I'm here to help find the truth. Wherever that leads us."

Fiona's eyes lit up. "Are you talking about a séance?"

"Count me in," Amber added.

Gabriel smiled at their enthusiasm. "It's not quite a séance. At least not in the way you ladies are thinking."

"What then?" asked Kelly, uncertain.

"I get psychic impressions. Sometimes spirits come to me, and I'm able to interpret what they're trying to say. But it's not like they speak through me; that's a Hollywood movie thing."

"Okay." Kelly breathed a bit easier. "That sounds—good."

"What now?" Fiona was ready for action.

Gabriel turned his full attention back to Kelly. "We need to go to a place where the connection between you and your sister is strong. And I'll need to hold something that belonged to your sister. Maybe a photo of her."

"We could go to the Los Feliz home. I'm moving out and will probably sell it soon. But she spent a lot of time there."

An hour later, Kelly steered her new Mercedes past the For Sale sign and through the gates of the Los Feliz estate. Gabriel followed in his Porsche, and Fiona and Amber pulled up behind him in Fiona's Honda Civic. The mansion's gates closed behind them and Kelly led the group inside the stately mansion.

Amber caught sight of the swimming pool and gardens in the back. "I'd never want to move out of this place, that's for sure." She turned to Kelly. "If you're leaving this, I can only imagine what your new condo must be like."

Kelly smiled politely and gestured toward the living room. "Please make yourselves comfortable, and I'll get us some wine."

"Let me help," offered Fiona as she followed Kelly into the gourmet kitchen.

Kelly opened a bottle of wine for them and Fiona carried the tray of glasses into the living room. Kelly chose a framed photo from the collection on the grand piano in the music room, and then joined the others. She handed the photo to Gabriel and sat nervously next to him on the sofa.

Gabriel took in the surroundings, "Beautiful home. I can feel there's been a lot of love here." He paused and closed his eyes. "Hmmm...there's also been great resentment...a lot of anger."

Kelly nodded, sadly. "I'm sorry to say that my sister and I never really got along. And her drug problem..."

Gabriel, eyes still closed, held up his hand to stop her. "Drugs aren't the issue I'm picking up on."

He moved his hands back and forth across the twins' photo and breathed deeply. The women watched in rapt silence as he entered a trance-like state. His hand began to move rapidly across the photo. "So much anger. Something terrible..." His hand moved faster, back and forth across the photo. "Hidden. Dead—"

Kelly stood up abruptly. "Stop. Please."

But Gabriel's hand kept moving back and forth across the picture. "Unhallowed ground..."

"Stop! She's dead!" Kelly cried. "I don't want to know anymore."

A loud crash echoed through the room and Amber screamed. Gabriel snapped out of his trance, slightly disoriented. Kelly rushed toward the sound, and the others followed her into the music room. A portrait of the twins had fallen from its place above the mantel. A ragged tear slit Jill's face in half, even though nothing appeared to have pierced the canvas during the fall.

Amber was so frightened she could barely manage a whisper. "It's your sister."

"It can't be..." Kelly's eyes were wide as she pulled her gaze from the portrait and turned toward Gabriel.

The psychic quickly moved to investigate. He closed his eyes and gently ran his hand across the tear. After a moment he turned to the women. "She's gone." Gabriel looked directly at Kelly. "I don't feel her presence anymore."

Kelly nodded as Gabriel carefully leaned the portrait against the wall. Fiona and Amber wanted to stay and keep Kelly company, but she insisted they leave. The other women reluctantly departed, and Kelly rejoined Gabriel.

The psychic appeared troubled. "Your sister is dead, but she's not at peace. As I said, I don't 'talk' to spirits; I get impressions. And I kept getting the image of unhallowed ground." Gabriel gently touched Kelly's arm. "I doubt she'll come back to me. I sense she only wants to talk to you. I don't think your sister can rest until you find her and bury her properly."

Kelly walked Gabriel outside to his car and gave him a quick kiss on the cheek. "Thanks."

"I don't think I did much."

"You helped me find the truth. Now I understand that I've got to find my sister somehow and help her rest in peace."

"Good luck with your search." He slid into his car. "I hope you find peace, too."

"Thanks." As soon as Gabriel was out of sight, Kelly ran inside, grabbed a water bottle and emptied it into the sink. Fifteen minutes later, she snuck into Incarnation Catholic Church in Glendale, filled the bottle with holy water, and headed for the Angeles National Forest.

High in the mountains, on one of the lonelier roads shooting off the highway, Kelly pulled to a stop beside a steep overlook. Halfway down the hill, almost completely hidden by the trees, she saw the small glint of metal visible from the remains of her sister's crashed car.

"Hey, sis," she called out to the silent mountain. "I need you to leave me alone once and for all. Not sure I believe in God, but apparently you do." She held up the bottle. "This is holy water, so it should do the trick. I'm not coming down there, so you'll have to make do with my sprinkling it on the hillside." She opened the bottle and started to pour holy water over the edge. "I'm sure a drop or two will hit you."

"That's your problem. You always were too lazy to do things right."

"Kelly?!" The twin dropped the bottle of holy water and spun around to find her sister pointing a gun at her. A cascade of brown curls gently blew in the mountain breeze.

"Hi, Jill. Surprised I'm not dead?"

"This isn't possible." Jill pulled nervously at her short blonde hair. "How...?"

The real Kelly shook her head. "You just couldn't wait around to see if I actually died after you drugged me and sent the car over the edge." Kelly raised the gun. "Trust me, I won't make the same mistake."

Unexpectedly, a Porsche pulled up behind them and Jill was relieved to see Gabriel get out.

"Gabriel!" She ran to him. "Thank God. I never believed that psychic stuff before but now..."

"Are you kidding?" Gabriel laughed and shook his head.

Jill's brain scrambled to process the situation as he stepped away from her and walked over to Kelly.

"Think about it. If your sister's actually alive, I never connected with her 'spirit,' did I?"

"When I came to after the crash," Kelly explained, "I spent hours crawling my way up the hillside. Gabriel was hiking that day. He heard my cries and rescued me."

Gabriel kissed Kelly and put his arm around her waist. "We've been together ever since."

"And when I set up your 'haunting,'" added Kelly, "I was curious to see if you regretted killing me. You didn't."

"Why would I?" Jill was defensive. "I asked for your help and—"

"I gave it to you. Over and over."

"Rehab," Jill spat out. "That's what you gave me over and over. I didn't need another rehab. I had things under control. I needed money, and you wouldn't give that to me."

"So you stole my life and everything in it?"

"You gave me no choice." Jill raised her chin, defiant. "And let's face it, I live your life better than you. I look better." She pointed to her short hair. "You'll never pull this off."

"Unlike you, my dear Jill, I pay attention to details." Kelly pulled off the dark wig, revealing an identical blonde pixie cut. "It's time to reclaim my life."

"Now what?" The tremor in Jill's voice belied her bravado. "I know you're not capable of doing it. You can't kill your own sister."

"Didn't you hear? Jill's already dead." Kelly took a step forward and pushed her twin off the cliff.

PALIMPSEST
Micheal Kelly

Kate Elliott fished a thirty-dollar bottle of pinot grigio from her refrigerator. "I earned this." It had taken hours to schlep inventory from her cargo van into the studio, and now, she filled a coffee mug with wine and walked through the house, turning off lights, locking doors, heading for the back bathroom.

LAPD helicopters thrummed overhead.

The neighbor's chihuahua yapped.

Kate said, "Get in the house, Rupert. It's coyote time."

She started the hot water and dumped bath beads into the tub. Glamorous antique dealer? Really? A façade that concealed hours of packing, loading and unloading.

Kate cut the lights and closed the bathroom window against the Silver Lake soundtrack. She peeled sweaty clothes from sticky skin, then stepped into the hot water.

Droplets formed and dripped down forest green tiles. Lavender steam blanketed the sourness emanating from the pile of clothes she'd left on the floor.

"Bubble bath should be a business expense." She draped a hot washcloth over her face and reviewed the weekend. Her receipts from three days' antique sales totaled just over nineteen thousand dollars. Most of it was promised as partial payment for the estate of a former client.

Exhaustion and wine wove a cocoon of drowsiness.

Her eyelids drooped. The pause between breaths lengthened.

Outside her bathroom window, gravel crunched.

She startled, found herself in the bath. Fallen asleep. Again.

The bath water was cool, and—

There it was again...the crunch of gravel.

She froze, straining to hear the faintest sound, hoping to hear silence.

Gravel crunching. Closer now.

Her heart raced.

Slowly...cautiously...she lifted herself out of the tub. She yanked a ratty black bathrobe from the door hook. Pushed wet arms into the sleeves. Ran to her bedroom. She peeked past the curtains.

Someone in dark clothes—a man?—was kneeling beside her van.

Lightheaded, Kate dropped to the carpet, crawled to the bureau and grabbed her cell phone.

She tapped nine-one-one.

"You have reached the Los Angeles Police Department," an automated voice announced. "An operator will be with you shortly."

"Are you freaking kidding me?" Kate peeked out the window again. Her throat constricted.

He?—*yes, it has to be a he*—was working the lock on the van's side door. It didn't take long—the burglar slid the van's door open and raked a penlight across the interior.

Empty.

He—*definitely a he, wide shoulders, narrow hips*—slid the door closed and crept toward the back of the house.

Where is Rupert? Why isn't he barking? Did he hurt Rupert?

Phone to her ear, Kate crawled to the far side of her bed and reached for the baseball bat she kept there. One of those eighteen-inch souvenir bats from a Dodger game. She froze in dismay at her foolishness. *Oh Lord, this is no weapon.* She crouched in the corner, hoping to hear a human on the phone, dreading the sound of the man outside.

"Nine-one-one operator, what is your emergency?"

Mind racing, Kate whispered, "There's a man outside my house. 1882 Silver Lake Boulevard. Please hurry."

"A unit's on the way. Is anyone with you?"

"I'm—"

Glass shattered.

Kate froze but managed to say, "Alone. I'm alone."

Glass crunched against wood floor in the studio. "Oh God, he's inside!"

"Get to a room where you can lock the door. Turn on the lights. I'm staying with you until officers arrive."

Eventually, the creak of footsteps and slamming of cupboard doors receded as wailing sirens screamed up Silver Lake Boulevard. Moments later, a police cruiser's red and blue lights raked her bedroom through the curtains. Kate remained frozen in the corner between the bed and the wall. *What if they shoot at him? Can bullets go through walls?*

Heavy footsteps pulverized glass. "LAPD!"

Rupert was back on the job, barking viciously on the other side of the fence.

The bedroom door knob rattled. "LAPD!"

A woman's voice came from the phone. "Ma'am? Ma'am! Officers are in your house. Tell me where you are."

Kate was asleep on the living room sofa when the doorbell rang. She bolted upright. Her baseball bat and butcher knife fell to the floor. She crept to the front door and peered through the peephole.

The man on the other side held up a badge.

She straightened her T-shirt, combed her hair with her

fingers and opened the door.

He stood two feet from the locked screen door, hands at his sides. "My name is David Gonzalez. I'm a detective with the LAPD." He looked like retired football player dressed in a Men's Wearhouse suit.

Kate waved him into her living room, a mid-century modern space with a floor-to-ceiling glass wall with a view of the reservoir. She stepped back to let the detective pass, and snuck a look at her watch. Already noon. Twelve hours since the uniformed officers left.

"Sorry I couldn't get here sooner." He sat in one of the black leather armchairs and pushed a stack of magazines to the edge of her coffee table. After opening a leather portfolio, he removed a copy of the police report she'd signed last night and placed both on the table.

Nervous, Kate still stood by the door. "Would you like water or...?"

He nodded. "Thanks. It's another hot one."

Kate walked through the dining room toward the kitchen and froze. The burglar's smell lingered in the back of the house. Cigarette smoke, unwashed clothes and sweat. She opened the window.

Hands shaking, ice cubes rattling, she carried two glasses of water to the living room.

Detective Gonzalez accepted one of the glasses, then opened his notebook. "Now, according to the report, the intruder first tried to burglarize your vehicle. Is that right?"

She nodded. "He was next to my van. But about fifteen minutes before that, the neighbor's dog started barking."

"He—it was a man, then?"

Narrow hips. Wide shoulders. The odor of his sweat. She said, "Yes."

"Describe him?"

"He was taller than me. The top of his head came to the van's roof." She stood and put her hand over her head. "Thin.

Wide shoulders. Dark pants, dark long-sleeved T-shirt, dark baseball cap..." She dropped back into the chair and picked up her glass. She tried to drink and nearly gagged.

Detective Gonzalez scribbled in his notebook. "Says here he broke into the van. Did he take anything?"

"Not from the van. I emptied it yesterday..."

"So, a dog barked. You looked out the window..."

"No. I was taking a bath." She hugged her waist and crossed her legs. "I fell asleep and something woke me and then I heard footsteps. I ran to the window and saw him at the van and then...he came toward the house..."

"Where were you? When you saw him."

"In my bedroom. Then...Then I heard glass breaking on the service porch. I locked my door and hid until the police got here." *Trapped in my bedroom like a chicken in a cage. It took them forever.*

Gonzalez flipped to a clean page in his notebook. "You told Officer Raskin that some business property was stolen."

She nodded. "Yes. A box of books."

Gonzalez blinked and looked up at her. "You're an antique dealer?"

She recognized the skepticism that flashed across his face. She'd seen it a hundred times when customers looked at a price tag.

"Yes. I deal in glass. Art glass, mostly."

"Art. Glass. And a burglar wants to steal...art glass. No offense."

"No offense taken." She delivered her three-minute lecture on glass and dropped a few buzz words: Tiffany, Murano, Lalique, Steuben.

"Tiffany. I heard of Tiffany." He clicked his pen. "But the stolen property list says...antiques books, value eleven hundred and fifty dollars?"

"Maybe he just grabbed a box when he heard the sirens?" She looked toward her studio, her throat now as dry as papyrus.

"Tell me about the thousand-plus dollars' worth of books." He looked down at the report to hide a smirk.

She could see the top of his head. Balding. "I did an antique show at the Pasadena Center last weekend. Besides glass I offered fifty books from the collection of a client named Sam Barbieri. He died six months ago. He looked like Luciano Pavarotti—twinkling eyes, huge stomach, talked with his hands."

Detective Gonzalez nodded. He clenched his jaws to stifle a yawn.

She took a sip of water, then continued. "Sam collected glass and books. He was a scholar of Renaissance Italian Art and professor at UCLA. A month ago his nephew called."

The detective sat up. "Nephew?"

She nodded. "His name is Jimmy Barbieri. Jimmy offered to sell me Sam's glass collection, but only if I would buy his books too."

"That's where the books come in?"

"I offered thirty of them last weekend. Those are the ones stolen last night."

"All thirty?"

"No. I sold seven."

Detective Gonzalez scribbled rapidly. "When you sell stuff, you write receipts?"

"Definitely. Names, addresses, phone numbers for everything sold."

"Can I see them?"

"Sure." Kate hurried to her studio, opened the center drawer of a mahogany partner's desk, and grabbed the receipts from the past weekend.

A moment later, she returned and set them on the coffee table. "You can keep these. I'll print another set."

"Thanks. Did last night's burglar look like any of the people who bought from you?" He pushed the receipts towards her.

She thumbed through the collection and set aside all the female buyers. "Tony Shaffer uses a wheelchair. Ethan McKenzie is a dead ringer for Danny DeVito. Not him. Not him..." Kate paused. "This one's not a regular customer—Steve Tanner. He bought a book of Italian poetry. Looks like Keanu Reeves."

Gonzalez wrote a note on Tanner's bill, then slid the receipts into his portfolio. "That's all I need for now." He stood and offered her his card. "Call me if you think of anything else."

A moment later, Kate stood at the window and watched Gonzalez steer his Crown Victoria down the hill. Once she could no longer see the blur of the red brake lights, she took a deep breath, then said, "No time like the present."

Out on the service porch, a hot Santa Ana wind blew through the broken window pane. She flinched as glass crunched underfoot or crashed into the waste basket, but she kept sweeping. Next, she dissected a corrugated box to thumb-tack over the door's gaping wound.

Her cell phone chirped. It was her handyman. "Thanks a bunch for calling back so quickly. I need a rush repair to my back door, and some shelves built for a walk-in closet. As close to yesterday as you can manage?"

That business handled, she tuned her Bose to classical radio and opened the studio's windows to clear the room of the burglar's smell. Rupert gave a friendly yap, mourning doves cooed, and orange blossom perfume wafted in on heated air. Mountains and beaches, museums and nightlife, cuisine of a hundred ethnicities.

There's no place like home.

Kate searched the drawers for three tiny silver bells her mother had tied to a birthday gift. Mom's definition of antique. Kate's idea of old-timey. "There you are, my pretties." She snipped a foot of slender black cord, threaded it through the bells, and hung it on the inside knob of her back door. A talisman. An alarm.

Was he one of the glass buyers? A neighborhood thief? An

agent of that oily book seller on La Brea?

"Let Gonzalez figure it out," she muttered. "You've got books to price." She pulled her hair off her neck, wound it through a scrunchie, and began sorting Sam's collection.

How much for *Pisa Illustrata?*

How much for *I Sessanta Cesarei?*

"I'm out of my depth." Who could she call?

Alfred Bergstrom was a book dealer. Expert, honest, helpful. Always so helpful.

Alfred was born the year the Hindenburg disaster horrified America. Kate hugged him and kissed both cheeks. The aroma of his pipe tobacco lingered on his jacket. She led him through the house, her hand at his elbow to steady him.

"...and when I said 'graphic novel' is an oxymoron, my grand-daughter unzipped her backpack. Out spilled every graphic novel written by Philip K. Dick! I was set up," he chuckled. He hung his gilt-handled cane—once owned by Mark Twain—on the studio's door knob, and lowered himself into the club chair.

A chilled bottle of Chardonnay was already uncorked. "Napa Valley 2015" Kate waggled the wine. She held up two wine glasses. "Target, 2018." She ran through the story of the break-in, praised Rupert for trying to warn her, and hoisted her tiny baseball bat from the floor. "This is now my office bat. I bought a man-sized aluminum bat for the bedroom. Since I haven't heard anything from the detective—it's been six days—I called him. No rash of break-ins around here. I don't know why he picked me. Enough of my burglar story. Let me tell you about Sam Barbieri while you work." She heaved several boxes of books nearer his chair.

He dried his hands on his pants. Running his fingertips across the spines peaking from the box, he said "Delicious, aren't they?" His eyes sparkled.

Kate put an inventory on the table. "Titles, dates, descriptions. Most are in Italian or Latin. Some languages I didn't recognize. Many dates are in Roman numerals."

He plucked a pen, coke-bottle glasses, and a magnifying glass from his jacket pocket. He held the books so close to his glasses, they tapped his nose. He fanned the gilded edge of one book to reveal a scene of Rome and the Tiber River. "These fore-edge paintings are quite sought-after," he explained. A few books Alfred kept on the table, the rest Kate delivered to the closet shelves.

At last Alfred sat back, sighed, and handed Kate the book list. "My dear Katie, here are your prices and remarks." His tiny notes filled the margins like a floral frame.

Kate felt as if she had just witnessed an expert grading diamonds. "Would you consider a fifty-fifty consignment? I can't represent them adequately. Pick whichever you wish to take to your shop. I'll deliver the rest." She offered her hand to seal the proposal.

Instead of shaking her hand, Alfred kissed it, then clapped in delight. "Agreed! Except...Except this book." He lifted a white leather-bound volume from the table. It was so heavy his hands trembled and his blue veins bulged. "We'll need an expert. The pages are parchment, not paper. The text is handwritten, not printed. A codex."

Kate's eyebrows scrunched. "Okay..."

"Look closely. Here." He pointed to a shadowy mark at the top margin, then he traced a line down the middle of a page. "These faint characters are text. Greek text, I believe. Look again. Pale lines run perpendicular to the Latin." He turned to a page in the middle of the book. "And on this page is the outline of a diagram. The vellum was washed of old text. This is a palimpsest."

Kate leaned forward for a closer look. "A...what?"

"Palimpsest." The old man tapped the book's cover. "It was a strategy employed when parchment was dear. Like reusing marble from a derelict temple to build a castle wall."

Kate squinted at the book. "So, is the value in the visible text or in what was written and drawn before?"

"Either." The old man winked and added, "Value is in the eye of the beholder, wouldn't you say? Book lovers are an odd lot. Our expertise often surpasses our means. Some lust for the book, some lust for the profit." He struggled to lift the heavy volume onto the table. "A single leaf palimpsest from a seventh-century Quran auctioned at Christie's London fetched well over two million pounds."

Kate gawked at him, and then at the book. "Two million...?"

He stroked the palimpsest. "I'm not comfortable taking this. I have a friend—a rare book dealer—who reads Latin and Greek. I'll ask her to call you. I am as anxious as you to hear what she says."

Kate placed three dozen books into boxes and carried them to the front door. She returned to the studio, helped the old man to his feet, and handed him his cane. Together they walked slowly to the front door and out to the baking city. As he shuffled to the driver's side of his ancient Cadillac, she deposited the books on his back seat.

"Be careful on the curves, Alfred. People drive too fast going down this hill."

"And you be careful too, my dear."

"I keep the porch lights on and I'm never far from my baseball bats." She leaned through the driver's window to squeeze his hand. The scent of his cherry tobacco mingled with orange blossoms.

Kate had locked the doors and was latching her bedroom window when her phone vibrated across her bureau. She froze, realized it was a call, and relaxed. "Alfred? Are you okay?"

"I just spoke with Didi Rankovich." He sounded like a boy

with a new train set. "I told her about your palimpsest. She's intrigued. Katie, she lives in San Francisco but she's in Pasadena right now, working on a project at the Huntington Library. She wants to visit you tomorrow morning."

"Alfred, you're a prince. Let me write down her..." From the corner of her gaze, she spotted movement outside the window.

There, beneath the bushes. She held her breath, moments away from hanging up on Alfred and calling the—

A skunk. It's just a...skunk.

The next evening Kate called Alfred to let him know that she'd met with Didi. No answer, so she left a message. "I wish you'd been here! She used an ultraviolet light and read some erased text. The Greek is about the Parthenon. Did you know it was a temple dedicated to Athena the virgin, and the Christians converted it to a church they re-dedicated to the Virgin Mary? I'll tell you all about it when you call back."

Kate repeated the word "palimpsest." She conjured images of Constantinople and Greek icons and incense and the great library at Alexandria. Palimpsest. Palimpsest.

A day passed with no call back from Alfred.

And then, another day.

And another.

Kate's jumpiness from the burglary waned while her anxiety for Alfred waxed. Maybe he was attending an antiquarian book fair. Maybe the grandkids were up from San Diego. Maybe...maybe she'd pop over to his shop.

She filled five plastic storage bins with Sam Barbieri's books and loaded them into her van. The drive to Bergstrom's in Larchmont Village was an easy shot down Silver Lake to Beverly Boulevard. Alfred lived above his business in an enviable old craftsman. Built-in bookcases, oak wainscoting, original leaded glass windows and a deep covered sitting porch for clients. He had once invited her to his second-floor retreat. It was a magic cavern. Antique maps and hand-colored engravings decorated his walls. His pipe collection snuggled in a revolving walnut bookcase next to an overstuffed wing chair. His only nod to the twentieth century was an electric stair lift.

She parked a block away on Beverly Boulevard and activated the van's alarm on her key fob. She ducked into La Cave, bought wine, a baguette and several cheeses, then walked to his shop.

A black sedan was parked in front of Bergstrom's. Short antennae bristled from its roof and trunk. The shop door stood open. An ambulance was in the driveway. Cops in black uniforms stood on the reading porch. The crackle of patrol car radios filled the air.

Kate stopped halfway down the street. She examined each piece of the jigsaw puzzle, but rejected the meaning.

Then she needed to know. Know that Albert was okay. She hurried toward the flashing lights.

A uniformed officer blocked her entry. "Sorry, ma'am. You can't enter."

"What? Why?" She strained to see into the shop's dark interior. "What's wrong? Is Alfred okay?"

He looked at the clear plastic bag in her hands. Inventoried its contents. Wine. Bread. Something else. "Are you a friend of Mr. Bergstrom?"

"Yes, yes...?" Nervous now, she looked past the cop.

"There's been a break-in." He took a breath. "I'm sorry. Your friend is dead."

Kate swayed. The bag fell to the sidewalk. Glass shattered. The policeman put an arm around her waist, and caught her before she collapsed.

A detective walked her to the nearest patrol car and helped her sit in its front seat. Then, he offered a brief story of the call. "...customer looked through the window...ransacked... bottom of the stairs...dead for three days..."

"Dead? Three days...? " she whispered, eyes wide.

The detective told her she could sit a while until she was ready to get up. He handed her his card.

She stared at the scene. *Alfred. Dead. Three days.*

She gripped the steering wheel and drove. Tenacious. Like a woman twice her age.

Sidewalks were clogged. Young brown men pushed ice cream handcarts. Old brown men in hats and cowboy boots stood on corners holding poles, anchoring balloons and cotton candy. Cars honked. Bicycles darted. Too many people.

She managed to reach home without causing an accident.

Parked, she turned off the ignition. The engine ticked. Sweat drenched her underarms. Rupert barked. A police helicopter circled above. Normal life in Silver Lake. *No. This is not normal. Nothing has been normal since the break-in. Nothing will be normal again.*

Still she sat. Imagining Alfred. Trying not to imagine his last moments. She put her hand to her mouth when she visualized him, all alone. Gone for three days.

Unsteady, she climbed the service porch stairs and unlocked the door. Her mother's bells tinkled. The house was cool and dark. She retreated to her studio. Dropped her purse onto the desk. Walked to the chair where Alfred had sat.

A hand covered her mouth. An arm cinched her neck.

She tried to scream, tried to claw his hand, but he was stronger. The stench of stale clothes and cigarettes poisoned the air.

He growled, "Shut up. Not a sound. I'm not going to hurt you." He dropped his hand from her mouth. "Where are the books?"

Kate screamed, a piercing shattering scream. She stomped her heel on his foot.

He howled and yanked her hair.

She fell backward, striking her head on the table before hitting the floor.

He sat on her chest and pinned her arms under his knees. He wore a black knit ski cap but she recognized his smell. And his eyes—Keanu Reeves eyes. Tanner?

He crushed his forearm against her throat.

She tried to turn her head. She thrashed and bucked, and crimson blackness closed around her. She forced herself to go still. She looked at him with terror, pleading with her eyes for her life.

He leaned forward until his beard scratched her jaw. "You don't want me to hurt you, do you?"

She shook her head.

"Ready to talk?" His voice rasped like a cold chisel on concrete.

She nodded, eyes wide.

"Where are they?" His lifted his arm from her throat.

Her lungs burned. She gasped. "Closet."

He stood. "Turn over. Forehead on the floor. Hands over your head. All the way up. All the way!"

She obeyed. *What is he going to do to me?*

She heard the closet door open and the light switch click.

Books crashed to the closet floor.

"It's not here. Where is it?" He knelt on her back. "The old book. The big white one."

Kate's tears soaked the carpet. He was still on her. *Can't breathe.* She pointed to her desk.

He got up and began yanking the drawers, sweeping his hands deep into the back of each one. He tossed her laptop to the floor. Pens, papers, price tags, postcards. All flung to the floor.

He said, "Yes," and pulled the palimpsest from the lower right drawer. He dropped to his knees to cradle the heavy text into his black backpack.

Kate spotted the baseball bat. *Now!* She grasped the bat

and rose to her knees. She swung blindly, striking his ankle.

He cried out and toppled sideways, crashing into her desk.

Kate leapt up and swung again, this time connecting with his side. His ribs crunched and the bat vibrated in her hands.

He grunted a single "oomph" as she drove the bat into his kidneys. Down he went, no longer moving.

Detective Gonzalez stood on Kate's front porch. "May I come in?"

Kate opened the screen door. "Detective."

He paused, taking in the bruise on her throat, then sat on the living room sofa. He set his portfolio on the coffee table and opened his mouth to ask his first question.

Kate, though, held up a hand. "That man. Was it Steve Tanner?"

"Yes."

"Did he kill Alfred?"

"We're still investigating."

She leaped to her feet and screamed at him. "I gave you the invoice! I gave you Tanner's address! Did you go there? Why didn't you stop him!"

"I'm sorry for your loss."

She slapped her hand on her thigh. "Can you tell me anything about Tanner? Can you tell me one single thing about Alfred Bergstrom's murder?"

Gonzalez shifted on the sofa and studied the notes in his portfolio. He sighed, then looked up at her. "We found a list of books at Bergstrom's shop. The list had Sam Barbieri's name on it, and yours. We took Jimmy Barbieri to the hospital. He recognized Tanner, and said Sam hired him to inventory his Latin books. Tanner kept asking if there were other books, and if Sam had ever seen a book about a sixth century bishop.

"Tanner is a teaching assistant and doctoral student at UCLA. I looked him up and interviewed the people in his department after your first break-in. They say he's convinced that there two books—one in Greek that lists the treasure of the Parthenon, and another in Latin about a Sicilian bishop who served at the temple in Athens. He thinks he can find that treasure if he can just find both books. The UCLA staff is convinced he's chasing unicorns."

Kate froze. "Alfred put it together. Alfred protected me." She swiped at the tears in her eyes, then motioned for the detective's pen and portfolio. She wrote down the name and phone number for Didi Rankovich on one of her business cards. "Give this woman a call. She examined the book, the one Tanner had in his backpack. He was right. Except there's only one book, not two. It's a special kind of book. A palimpsest."

Detective Gonzalez said, "Okay," and then, "We may need to get some photographs of that book after we talk to Rankovich."

A tear tumbled down Kate's cheek. "I don't have it. I don't want anything more to do with it. After you talk to Didi Rankovich, you can go over to UCLA to see the palimpsest. I've donated all of Sam Barbieri's books to their library, in the name of Alfred Bergstrom."

BLOOD SHADOWS
B.J. Graf

When Paul Myrtilos saw the two men in off-the-rack suits walking up the driveway to the house in Reseda where he lived with his sister Thea, he grabbed his keys and slipped out the back. The bulges under the left arm of their suit jackets from the guns holstered there told Paul they were detectives. Had he seen the bow-legged one in the shiny brown suit poking through his trash a week ago? Paul couldn't be sure, but he wasn't going to wait and see.

Two uniformed cops sat in a squad car, which they'd parked in front of his garage to block entry and exit. Paul smiled and shook his head. He'd parked his white van on a side street half a block away in case the cops ever paid him such a visit. Now, in the gloom before sunrise, he slipped through a neighbor's yard like a shadow.

Paul climbed into his Ford van and drove off. He turned right onto the Ventura Freeway and headed east. Paul Myrtilos liked to wake up early and pilot his van along the miles of open road running through the city like black arteries. It calmed him down after a hunt. Normally.

Now, tapping the steering wheel with impatient little jabs, Paul's van crawled east along the 101. The bumper-to-bumper traffic moved so slowly it wasn't long before his right foot ached from riding the brake. Must be an accident. His kid sister Thea had told him Los Angeles had won the award for worst traffic in the U.S. for two years in a row. Thea was a few cards short of a deck—she'd believed him when he'd sold her a lie about her being adopted. But she tended to get facts like stats on traffic right.

When he passed Van Nuys, Paul spotted the black and white riding his tail. He didn't break a sweat, even when he exited the freeway at Laurel Canyon Boulevard with the cop car still on top of him. When Paul turned left on Ventura, heading east towards Hollywood, the bar of colored lights on the cop car began to flash.

Running was pointless now, so Paul kept his cool and pulled over to the curb. He glanced in the rearview mirror and waited for the cops to approach. He smoothed back his well-cut salt and pepper hair, ran his tongue over his teeth, and popped a breath mint into his mouth. He then directed his gaze at the approaching blue-suiters.

The female officer was a fine-boned brunette with amber eyes and a lot going on beneath her uniform. Exactly his type if he'd been on a hunt. Paul handed over his license and registration with a smile. Maybe, just maybe this was a routine traffic stop, unrelated to the two detectives who'd paid him an unscheduled visit this morning.

"What's the problem, Officer Jimenez?" he said, reading her nametag. Paul knew his papers were in order, and he never called attention to himself by speeding or reckless driving.

"Would you step out of the vehicle and open the back of the van please."

Paul complied. She'd find nothing in the van except dog hair from his sister's black lab. No law against that. Paul didn't begin to worry until he saw the flash of silver as the cop pulled out her set of handcuffs.

"Turn around and place your hands on the roof of the vehicle."

"Why? I wasn't speeding." Paul forced himself to stay calm.

"Paul Myrtilos, you're under arrest for the murder of Daria Reyes," Officer Jimenez said as she slapped the cuffs on Paul's hands and read him his rights.

Damn. Daria Reyes. She'd been the redhead. He waited, but the Jimenez bitch didn't mention any of the others. And there'd been twenty-seven others.

"You've made a mistake," Paul said, still smiling, as Officer Jimenez and her partner tucked him into the squad car for the ride to the station.

Mistakes. In the twenty-five years he'd been on the hunt, Paul had only made one. It was that stupid mutt that made him do it. If that dog had just kept quiet, Paul wouldn't have left that used condom in the redhead's apartment. He was usually so fucking meticulous. Paul had taken out all the security cameras even though he wore a wig and gloves and always burned his clothes afterward. And as for his girls, Paul was careful to wash the bodies in a good bleach solution and comb even their pubic hair to make sure he hadn't left any trophies for the cops to find. But the redhead's dog had kept barking, and that made Paul shoot the mutt in order to shut it up. Right through its throat. The shot woke up the neighbors. So, he'd had to rush through his checklist. He'd set the rubber on the counter, meaning to flush it down the toilet, but he hadn't.

That was a year ago, and for the first six months after he'd made that mistake, it haunted his every waking moment. There wasn't a day that went by where he didn't wake up and curse his bad luck. It made him short-tempered, and that made him sloppy. He'd shot Thea's black lab that one time when she went away for the weekend when its barking got under his skin. What had Thea called that dog? Snowball. That was it. What a dumb name for a black lab. At any rate, he'd bought her another dog because she wouldn't stop bawling like a baby.

Now as Officer Jimenez marched him past the giant fingerprints etched into the walkway that led to the entry of the North Hollywood Police Station, Paul began to calm down. They took his phone and brought Paul into an interview room. Officer Jimenez removed the cuffs as a scruffy thirty-something detective entered the room. It was the bow-legged cop in the shiny brown suit from this morning.

"You led us on quite a chase, Mr. Myrtilos," the scruffy detective said. He introduced himself as Detective Frank Waldron.

Unlike Paul, who kept himself fit and well-groomed, Waldron was twenty pounds overweight and had stains on his tie.

"I don't know what you're talking about." Paul looked around the room. There was nothing to see besides the grey walls behind the two chairs and the plain table between them. "I often take long drives in the morning. No law against that, is there?" He took a deep breath to center himself. The air smelled like stale coffee and disinfectant.

"No," Detective Waldron said as he began to lay out pictures on the table between them. "No law against that."

The photos showed crime scenes with those little yellow markers the crime techs used. In one of the real old photos, there was a chalk outline to show where the body had once lain. Blood shadows. Cops used to call those chalk outlines blood shadows.

"Would you like a cup of coffee?" the detective said. He began to lay out more pictures, graphic crime scene photos with the bodies still in them this time.

"No, thanks." Paul made sure he didn't smile when he glanced at the pictures. He forced himself to look a little shocked at all the blood.

From the photos, Paul knew the cops suspected he'd done these other girls, some of them at least. He counted four besides the redhead, not the twenty-seven he'd actually killed. But they'd only charged him with the Reyes murder.

Paul bit his lip. Detective Waldron was bluffing. They probably had the condom Paul had left in the redhead's apartment by mistake, but nothing else. Since his DNA wasn't in the system, they'd need a court order to force a sample from him to match the DNA found in the condom. That took time, and Paul planned to get out of Los Angeles by then. He certainly wasn't going to give the cops a saliva sample on a coffee cup now and incriminate himself.

When Paul refused the coffee, the detective placed a plastic bottle of water in front of Paul. "Water? The AC has been on the fritz all week."

The air in the room did feel hot, hot and stuffy. Paul wondered if they'd turned off the AC on purpose to make him sweat. He'd read cops did stuff like that. He refused to touch the water.

"I'm afraid you've made a mistake," Paul said. "I don't know why you think I had anything to do with this." He gestured to the pictures.

"We've known for a while someone with a genetic profile similar to yours murdered Daria Reyes, Mr. Myrtilos. Somebody in your family. It took some time to narrow down the suspects to you."

"Someone in my family? What are you talking about?" Paul didn't have to force a shocked expression on his face this time. He really wanted that water now.

The detective pulled a sheet of paper out of his file, turned it around and pushed it forward so Paul could read it. It was a report from an open source genealogical website that allowed the public to send in DNA in order to trace ancestry. The name printed on the line that said "customer" was Thea Myrtilos.

Paul shook his head. What had his idiot sister done now? The report was dated April 2018. One year ago. He sighed. That was about the time he'd told Thea she'd been adopted. And the gullible fool had believed him. Believed him enough to do an ancestry search. Her DNA put a target on his back.

He told himself to stay calm. The cops only had a family

profile match. That didn't prove *he* did it. And he wasn't going to give them anything.

"I want a lawyer," Paul said.

"You'll need one," Detective Waldron said, nodding. "Daria Reyes isn't your only murder victim, is she?" He tapped each of the photos of the four women besides the redheaded Reyes in turn. "Tell us about the others. How many were there?"

Paul crossed his arms over his chest.

"You'll help yourself if you cooperate, Paul. Why don't we start by swabbing your cheek? We'd like you to give us a DNA sample, voluntarily."

"So you can frame me," Paul said. "I've heard about cops planting evidence. No way."

"Actually, it's for your own protection," Detective Waldron said. "We already have a sample from you that matches the DNA in the contents we found in a used condom inside Daria Reyes' apartment."

"What are you talking about?" Even as he said it, Paul knew. That's why Waldron had been poking around in his trash a week ago. He'd stolen Paul's DNA off a beer bottle or a clump of hair.

Paul swore a blue streak under his breath. He wasn't going to take this lying down. He would fight it. Paul wondered if he could get the DNA from his trash excluded from evidence somehow. He'd be sure to ask his lawyer.

"Your sister Thea's here with the lawyer," Detective Waldron said an hour after Paul had placed his one phone call. "You want to see her?"

Paul nodded.

A few minutes later they brought Thea into the interview room, without the lawyer. The cops probably hoped Paul would further incriminate himself.

"Your attorney will be right in," Detective Waldron said

from the door. "Thea wanted to talk with you alone for a minute. I'll get us coffee."

Paul's mousy-haired sister had bitten the cuticles around her nails until they bled, and the dark bags under her eyes had grown big enough to hide a small corpse. He waited until she had taken a seat opposite him before he started to unload.

"What did you do, Thea? What did you do?!"

"The police showed me the pictures," Thea said in a quiet voice as she stared down at her hands with the bloody cuticles. She wore that ratty old sweater he hated and hadn't even managed to button it right. Thea looked so much older than her thirty-seven years. "They said you killed those women."

"The only crime here is what you did, sending your DNA to that ancestry website. I'm your brother, Thea, and the cops are using it to frame me."

"You said you *weren't* my brother," Thea countered, her eyes still downcast. Tears fell from them. "That was the day you told me I was adopted. The day Snowball went away."

"That's because I was mad at you!" he yelled. "Because you do stupid things."

"Were you mad at Snowball too?"

"Snowball?" He stared at her. What did the idiot dog have to do with anything? "I told you before, Thea. I didn't do anything to that dog. He just ran off."

"No, he didn't," Thea said. "I found Snowball's body in the trash. In one of those cheap kitchen garbage bags you use. Somebody shot him. There was blood leaking out of the bag."

Paul closed his eyes for a second, then opened them again as he jabbed at the table between them. "Well, it wasn't me. I even got you a new dog, didn't I?"

Thea didn't answer. She looked different too, something about the set of her thin shoulders changed.

Paul forced himself to lower his voice and take a deep breath. He had to remember she wasn't too sharp, and he would need her to post his bail.

"Thea, I know you're upset," Paul said. "I don't blame you. None of this was your fault. I should never have said you were adopted. That was wrong. You were confused, so you sent your DNA to that website. I get it. But the cops used that to set me up, don't you see?"

"I'm not confused," she said, slowly raising her head and staring back at him. Her dark eyes had grown hard. "I was *hoping* the ancestry website would share information with the police."

Paul felt a trickle of cold sweat snake down his back as realization wormed its way into his head. "You didn't send your DNA to that website because you thought you were adopted?"

Thea shook her head. "I always knew we were tied by blood. Even if I hated the idea. I wasn't sure you killed those women at first, but the dates of their murders always matched the times you were gone. Then, after the Golden State Killer, I heard the police were checking genealogy sites. I knew there was a way to finally find out."

"You sent your DNA to the website to trap me?" Paul stared at his sister. It was like looking at a stranger.

Thea's eyes widened. "You trapped yourself, Paul. You shot Snowball through the throat. Just like you shot that woman's dog after you murdered her. Now you'll have to pay the price." She rose from her seat. She seemed much taller than her height of five feet, six inches.

"I didn't want it to be you." Thea looked down at him. "I kept telling myself I was wrong, that you couldn't be a murderer. Right up until today I kept telling myself that. Because you're my brother. My blood. The fact that we're related will haunt me to the end of my days. How I wish I were adopted."

When she reached the door to the interview room, his sister turned her back on him with a finality that felt like a judge's sentence. And the door closed behind her with a hollow clang.

STRANDS OF TIME
Roger Cannon

Monday morning, 8 a.m., Bell Gardens Police Department briefing room

"First name's Jake, last name's Revenir. Friends call me Rev. Not much to tell. I'm twenty-eight, graduated from B.G. High ten years ago and joined the military right away. Had two tours of duty in Afghanistan, one in Iraq. Special Forces trained me well." A few heads at the briefing wagged approval. "I left as a sergeant after six years, went to college four more, and got my Bachelor's in Police Science. What I learned overseas should serve me well as a police officer. I appreciate your consideration. Thanks."

Captain Fairchild then reviewed major crimes and misdemeanors that happened over the weekend. Ten minutes later, the meeting ended and officers shuffled to their lockers or squad cars to start their day.

"Rev, you're with me today for the ride-along. I'm Sergeant Rodriguez. Given name's Santiago, but everyone calls me Chago. Get your gear and meet me in the parking lot."

I'd heard about the handsome, thirty-five-year-old, bilingual officer with the thick black moustache who had been with the department ten years. Acclaimed as one of the few glues who held the city and the P.D. together, Chago's promotion to lieutenant was expected soon. To spend time with BGPD's finest, I would know by the end of the day if I would be a good fit here.

Five minutes later, I met Chago in the parking lot. "Rookie, we inspect the car every time before we set out to start a shift. It reduces screw-ups that can bite us in the butt later."

"Show me your routine, Sarge. You won't have to show me twice."

After a quick inspection of our 2016 Explorer, we drove to Eva's restaurant two minutes away and swung into an open booth.

Chago greeted both waitresses and waved to the cook. "Eva's coffee's way better than the station's, and they make a mean Acapulco omelet. We're in no hurry because I want to get to know you, so order away."

I placed my order, then scanned the room's patrons, slowly—one at a time—while Chago glanced at the menu.

"So, who's the biggest threat in the room, Rev?"

"The gangbanger on the aisle facing us in the last booth. His jitters and inability to focus makes me think he's a druggie. The tats on his neck and hands have 'prison' written all over him. Guys like him erupt easily if anyone pushes them." I paused for a moment. "On second thought, the most dangerous man in the room might be you, Sarge."

Chago's phone buzzed. He read the text aloud. "Over the weekend, a twenty-eight-year-old woman was beaten to death in town. The medical examiner estimated the time of death occurred Saturday evening. The body wasn't discovered until Sunday afternoon. Here's what we got."

Chago handed me the phone. I inspected two images of a crumpled, young woman in a pink bathrobe at the base of a broken wall mirror, her face puffy and bruised, her neck slit. Sticky blood spatters had landed everywhere.

"Who does heartless shit like this, Chago?"

"Happens more often than you'd think."

Without thinking, I stared at the young woman's death mask. My eyes watered as I recognized my ex-girlfriend, Vero.

"Can you forward me these photos? I liked to study crime-related photos when on active duty with Special Ops. We never knew what we might learn. Rod Stewart said it best, 'Every picture tells...a story, don't it?'" Chago finished the line. He took my cell phone and transmitted the photos from his. "What else would you like to know?"

I cracked my neck and exhaled. "Do you believe history repeats itself, Sarge?"

"I do. Your point is...?"

"Years ago, I had a professor who brought history alive for me when he talked about 'strands of time.'"

Chago looked bewildered. "What're you talking about?"

"He told the class to visualize a thick rope, the kind used to secure a boat to a landing. The rope had many strands, and each one disappeared as it braided along the unseen side of the rope, then reappeared again. The process was repeated again and again, from one end of the rope to the other."

Chago raised an eyebrow.

"He told us to imagine that rope represented 'history,' and its strands were made of time. If we don't learn from our mistakes over time, they'll come back to haunt us later, maybe in a different shape or circumstance."

"Chago, I been holding out on you. I just completed LAPD's training, and they want to hire me, but I grew up in town here, and I wanted to do a ride-along with you before I made up my mind who to sign with. I have a lot at stake. There's loose ends I *have to* tie up this morning, so I'm asking for a big favor. I'm asking you to believe in me, even though we've just met."

Chago's eyes bored into mine. He deliberated for a long moment, then spoke his truth: "Rev, ten years ago somebody asked me to believe in him, and I played it by the book. That didn't work out well. Then five years ago, I worked with a high school senior who had feet in two worlds, each straddling the line of the law—one heavy into graffiti and gang vendettas, the other into a career in law enforcement. I went with my gut for that kid when he needed me. Today he's a first-year LAPD officer doing a great job."

Chago stroked his moustache, then resumed our conversation, "And now here you are. I don't know your story, but my gut tells me it's worth hearing what you got to say. Our conversation won't go beyond this booth."

"Thanks, Chago. I won't let you down."

"One condition, rook—I call you, or you call me regularly. I can cover for you for a while, but it's serious shit if you go off the radar. Do you understand?"

"I do, Sarge. You have my word."

"Okay, let's box our food, and I'll drop you at your car."

Saturday, two days earlier, three p.m., Montebello Chevrolet, Whittier Boulevard

I hadn't seen her in a decade until we met at the ten-year Bell Gardens High reunion a week ago at the Rio Hondo Country Club. I wasn't sure why I had attended the event until I saw Veronica. She'd thrown a drink in the face of a vaguely familiar muscle-bound guy who had gangbanger written all over him. My buddy Zeke told me the guy, known as "Boxer," used to date Vero until she got tired of his bullshit. Boxer glared in our direction before management asked him to leave.

That was my cue to reconnect with my old flame. We'd been close the last half of our senior year. I abruptly ended it when I left for boot camp two days after graduation. Vero was hurt and angry because I excluded her from the conversation. We couldn't patch things up, and we drifted apart and moved on.

Ten years had passed, and the girl I knew then was a woman now. Seeing her re-lit a spark I thought had died. I didn't know where things would go, but deep down I longed for a second chance. Vero and I exchanged emails and texts the whole next week, intent on getting together.

We arranged to meet at the Chevy dealership where her new black Silverado truck was in for a tune-up, ready for pickup by seven p.m. A strange place for a first "re-connect," but I couldn't complain.

I drove up at three. Standing in front of the Chevrolet of Montebello dealership, Vero wore a Hot Pink lace up jumpsuit, and I do mean *hot*. Her black After Hours heels accented her well-turned ankles; her long, streaked blonde hair spilled over a shoulder, almost reaching her waist; Burberry sunglasses, Blue Nile gold looped earrings, and a stunning gold Irish claddagh pendant on her neck rounded out a beautiful young woman in prime time.

Vero stuck out her thumb like a hitchhiker. "Going my way, cowboy? I need a good ride."

"What'd you have in mind, señorita?"

"Give me a ride, homeboy, to my empty crib. It's an offer you shouldn't refuse."

"Hop in, *chica*."

Vero slid across the seat next to me. She had curves in places where most girls don't have places. "Glad you don't have bucket seats, baby. I hate climbing over those."

On the ride to her apartment, her left hand found my inner thigh, and my throat went dry. Vero pushed her *chichis grandes* forward as her hand moved slowly in the opposite direction. I saw hardened nipples tautly pushing against her hot pink jumpsuit.

The lines from Roy Hamilton's oldie lilted out of my '66 Chevy Impala's radio—"Ooh wee...this feeling's killing me/ Ah shucks, I won't stop for a million bucks..." Oldies music still creates a musical identity for many Chicanos in southern

California. We both laughed at the timing of the song lyrics.

She bragged, "Once upon a time, my street had eight gangs within a block's radius of my address. It's better now, but still a tough neighborhood. We're almost there. It's time you see my pad."

She pointed out her big apartment building on the right as we turned onto Quinn. I drove past her building and the large house next door shielded by two huge trees out front and continued another fifty yards further down the street, pulling over next to an empty parking lot.

Vero's eyes widened. "Why you parking way down here?"

"Good exercise." I'd learned a long time ago to: *Never park directly in front of where you'll be. Make anyone looking for your car have to guess where you are. Contingency plans are useful in varrios or ghettoes.*

Vero shrugged and slid out of the seat, right behind me. Out of habit, I scanned the neighborhood as we walked to her building. Kids played tag across the street, gardeners joked with each other as they clipped bushes at a neighbor's big, red-tiled property, and several women chatted and laughed together at the far end of Vero's apartment complex in front of a door marked Laundry.

"Follow me," Vero purred as she hip-switched up a flaking metal staircase.

"Whatever you say, *bonita.*"

Vero's keys unlocked a deadbolt, then a regular lock to open apartment 4B. Once inside, she secured both locks.

"Can't be too careful, Rev. Lots of break-ins around here."

Her apartment was as quiet as an old shoe and just as smelly.

"Okay if I open a window?" as I moved toward one across the living room. "It's stuffy in here."

"No problem. Gotta check messages. Be right back."

I opened a window in the living room and noticed a fire escape ladder six feet away, half the distance to her neighbor's apartment. It reminded me of people in Mosul who didn't get out of death traps like this when there was a fire.

I turned around, and Vero was there, putting arms around my waist and pulling me into her. She offered me her neck, which I gladly accepted. She moaned.

"Is someone coming home?"

"Not till six. Are you here to talk about my roomie or enjoy me?"

"Want to tell me about that big crack in the wall near the TV?"

"Compliments of my roommate, Lupe. Her street name's *Loca*, because she goes crazy when she's mad. And she's mad a lot of the time. Lupe's a big, tough chick with quick temper who loves to fight. Easy to see why she was in a gang for a long time."

"Has she threatened you?"

"Oh, yeah. She threw a vase at me two days ago and missed. I still owe her two months' rent, and she accused me of trying to steal her boyfriend. She's coming home tonight from her folks in Moreno Valley. I definitely ain't gonna be here when she shows up."

"She makes a big deal about money you owe her, Vero. Does she work?"

"Lupe's a very good tattoo artist. I know she does okay if she's not tweaking."

Vero had misted a light perfume across her shoulders and the back of her neck while in the other room. I tugged down a strap from her sexy jumpsuit. She fought me off, mischief in her eyes. "You're a *bad boy*!"

We traded tongues, then I returned to her neck, not pulling my face away until she moaned.

Out of the blue, Vero asked, "Hey, talking about bad boys, did you see the guy at the reunion I threw a drink at?"

A silent alarm went off inside me. "Why do you ask, *chica*?"

She knew she'd pushed too far too soon. Her tongue flickered in my ear, but I made her stop.

"Yeah, I recognized that asshole. My friends in high school didn't like him or his gang. We used to do some graffiti—you knew that—but hell, who didn't around here?" I said as I kissed her. "Are we done talking?"

Vero took my hand and pulled me toward her bedroom. "Get comfortable. I wanna take a quick bath. I feel grungy. It won't take long. You wait here." She pushed me into her bedroom and closed the door.

Two minutes later, bath water sounds came from somewhere down the hall. I got hungry and crossed the living room into the little kitchen where I treated myself to a handful of Raisin Bran.

Scanning the room for nothing in particular, I noticed the front door was ajar. "How'd that happen?" I asked myself as I re-locked it.

Three car doors creaked open outside. My combat instincts kicked in. I peered through the kitchen blinds to see three *cholos* piling out of a shiny black Camaro.

The driver, tall and skinny, wore dark brown chinos and looked familiar. "Hell, that's Ces, a *cabrón* from the old days. The backseat guy's Eighteenth Street, too."

A stocky guy with arms like Popeye's emerged from the shotgun seat and slammed his door hard. Boxer!

I pulled on my T-shirt and moved across the living room to the open window. Looking both ways—my lucky day—nobody in sight. I gauged in my head it was a twenty-foot drop straight down to the cement courtyard below. Bad option for a jump.

Vero hurried into the room in her bathrobe, clutching at my arm. I jerked it away. Tears in her eyes, she whispered, "Sorry, I'm so sorry, Rev. Boxer said I'd only attract guys with my body once he got done with my face if I didn't call him. I *had to* make the call." She looked at me wild-eyed.

"My looks are all I got, Rev. Please go." Vero sobbed as she retreated to the bathroom.

I saw a little piece of chalk on Vero's "Reminders" board and crushed it in my hands. Footsteps pounded down the corridor. Hard knocking began on her front door.

I talk to myself when stressed. "Keep hands dry so I won't slip." I climbed out the window, slowly reversing my body to face the building's exterior. With great care, I put my feet together onto the slanted little sill. Then, I straightened up slowly, holding the window's frame with my right hand. I started moving to my left two inches at a time, first with the left foot, then with the right.

The pounding outside the apartment's door increased while someone pushed the doorbell buzzer non-stop, but I only concentrated on the window ledge. I heard muffled footsteps inside the apartment as I leapt for the fire escape ladder. I missed the building's façade and gripped the ladder forcefully when my hands made contact. My adrenaline was off the charts. I decided to go up instead of down, reaching the roof seconds later.

I hotfooted it along the flat roof of the long building, away from the pounding of fists on wood and raised voices. The red-tiled roof of the large home next door presented a tough drop onto a nasty slant, so I kept moving along the roofline. Ten seconds later, the sloped tiled roof ended, and a flat, gray-shingled rooftop began, only six feet below where I stood.

No-brainer. I swung over the side, landing on the rooftop below and zipped across that roof at an angle to another rooftop only four feet below. Reminding myself to stay focused, stay agile, I sprang onto the new rooftop.

From one corner of the little rooftop, I spotted the rear end of a flatbed El Camino pickup truck protruding from a garage below. All that remained in my way out of this jam was a driveway beyond.

I hollered "Banzai" like I had in the days when I jumped

out of planes over enemy territory. I leapt, feet wide apart, only eight feet down onto the middle of the pickup's cargo bed, kangarooed off onto the driveway, and executed a forward roll as soon as my feet struck pavement. I imagined gymnastic judges holding up nines and tens on their cards for my acrobatics before I ran out the driveway leading to the street.

Somebody yelled from behind, "Hey, what you think you're doing, punk?"

I didn't bother to look back as I sprinted for my car. I imagined the shit Vero heard from her ex-boyfriend as I raced away. Then, I remembered the unlocked door...

Bell Gardens, Monday mid-morning

I drove to the murder scene, Vero's apartment building. Once parked, I looked at the selfies I had taken of Vero and me when she bought cigarettes at a liquor store on the way to her pad. We looked so happy. Then, I stared at the transmitted photos of her dead body. I stared at them and noticed something odd—no Irish pendant was visible on Vero's body.

I noticed yellow crime scene tape as I walked into the courtyard of her apartment building. The tenant mailbox listed "V. Lopez/L. Ortega" on the label for 4B. I took a pic with my cell phone, then pressed the mailbox button for the manager, "M Avakian." I got an answering machine. I left my number and a message, "This is Officer Revenir. I have some questions. Call me. It's important."

Two middle school boys peered at me through a crack in a door of a nearby unit. "Hey, guys, why aren't you at school?"

"It's Teacher Workshop Day," they said in unison. "No classes in the district today. Pretty cool, huh?" They opened the door a little more.

"You guys live here? I need some information."

"How much you got?"

We settled on twenty bucks.

They told me Saturday afternoon they saw Vero, looking hot, with a new guy. I breathed easier they hadn't recognized me.

One boy said, "Three gangbangers came around her place at four o'clock and made a lot of noise trying to get in. We heard lots of yelling, and things breaking. Then, they left. Lupe, the big mean chick who lives there, too, showed up around five or six. She drove off but came back later that night. She took boxes and boxes of stuff out to Vero's Silverado."

"Anyone else go up there, *chavalitos?*"

"The landlady came Sunday afternoon to collect the rent. When no one answered, she went inside. Everybody heard her scream, and she called the cops."

We fist-bumped, and I laid a twenty on them. The budding entrepreneurs high-fived each other and ran off.

I called the Chevrolet agency on Whittier Boulevard. After identifying myself to the manager, I asked if Veronica Lopez had collected her truck.

The manager said, "Her sister Lupe picked it up for her."

"When?"

"Saturday, before closing."

"Did she pay for the work with a credit card?"

"Let me look it up." A minute later, he came back on line. "Nope. She paid two hundred twenty-three dollars in cash. Is everything okay, Officer?"

"Yes, sir, just checking out a lead. Thanks for the help."

My cell buzzed. It was the manager of Vero's apartment returning my call. I listened to her complain that Vero died inside the apartment, and Lupe left, stiffing her and her husband two months back rent."

"Mrs. Avakian, we'd like to help you get your rent money, but I need Lupe's contact information in order to do it. Do you have a phone number for her family in Moreno Valley?"

She did. I scribbled the number down.

I needed to find Boxer and Lupe, confront them, and get the truth. My resources had run dry, except one. I'd be taking a chance of losing a career, and perhaps losing my freedom. Keep my yap shut, and I might walk away scot-free.

Back at the car, I wolfed down my boxed-up breakfast. Then, I punched in the numbers for Chago's cell. "It's Rev. I need your help."

"What is it, rook?"

"I need an address for a gang guy in town, street name Boxer. It's a part of my past I'm trying to clear up, and it's urgent. I'm asking you again to trust me. I got a lot on the line."

"Let me call you back."

Chago rang the department's gang unit. They knew Boxer. His jacket listed a felony assault and battery, resisting arrest, drunk and disorderly conduct, and a few lesser charges. They also had his most recent address, matching the one listed at the DMV.

Chago texted me. *Meet me in ten. Eva's parking lot.*

Ten minutes later, Chago motioned me to get into his squad car.

"I got Boxer's address. Now, what's this about?"

I exhaled, then recounted my connection to Vero, the homicide victim whose photos I first saw on Chago's phone. I told Chago about my narrow escape from her apartment on Saturday afternoon, and the gang guys wanting to harm me because of a long-standing vendetta. I brought the sergeant current on everything I'd done since I'd driven away from the station several hours ago.

Chago listened intently. "What's your connection to Boxer?"

I walked him through a high school fight where Boxer and two of his buddies had jumped me. We both knew gang guys sometimes did random attacks on people with no connection to them.

"When my dad passed away seven years ago, Mom told

me the *real* story. Boxer's old man had been hitting on her and harassing her at work. When Mom told my dad, he became enraged and got into a fight with Boxer's old man. Slammed his skull into a street curb. Killed him. Dad escaped clean and lived out a gang-free life, the one he'd promised Mom. But the story didn't go away, and his kid wanted vengeance. When Boxer saw me at the ten-year reunion, he knew I was in town."

"Rev, this is risky territory. We team up with the sheriff's department on homicides most of the time in our little town. We're almost at that point, but for now, I'm in. I want to see where this goes, so I'm coming with you."

Boxer's last known address was on Kress Avenue in a small, deteriorated Craftsman house, one of many jammed on a street filled with WWII-era homes. We drove fifty yards past the address and parked under a huge fichus tree. The street was empty for a mid-afternoon.

We both advanced quickly. Chago signaled for me to cover the back. Someone inside the house yelled, "Five-ohs!" as I moved along the side of the house. A screen door banged open at the rear of the house, and I caught sight of Boxer barreling toward a low fence separating his place and a neighbor's property.

Chago had kicked in the front door and gotten the drop on two gangbangers inside while I sprinted after Boxer. Boxer had a ten-yard lead as he crossed a neighbor's yard and continued out into the next street. He ran along the sidewalk until I tackled him from behind.

"You!" yelled the husky gangster clad only in a pair of *Boxer* shorts. "I been waitin' a lifetime for this." He extended his arms, palms up, fingers beckoning as he got to his feet, inviting me to fight.

I knew gang guys liked to "rush" victims, so Boxer's initial charge proved easy to sidestep. As a former Green Beret, I often used combat infighting techniques in physical altercations. It gave me an edge, one unknown to the powerful man standing before me.

I circled to Boxer's left, dukes up. I stepped inside, *pop-pop*, delivering two quick blows to Boxer's face before dancing back out of range. A moment later, we were at it, toe-to-toe, street boxing, *varrio* style. Neighbors spilled out of doorways to watch our *mano à mano* combat.

Boxer landed a hard right to my chest, knocking me off-balance for a moment. He charged clumsily at me. I switched in a heartbeat to battle-seasoned mixed martial art moves, delivering a pair of punches to Boxer's head that drew blood from his nose and lips. It was easy to avoid his wild haymaker swings. Boxer was in his zone, but out of his league.

I stepped inside the muscle-bound gangbanger and hammered him with two hard kidney punches, then executed a Bruce Lee sweep move to cut his legs out from under him. Boxer landed near a street curb. I pounced on him and slammed the back of his head hard into the curb. My combat training said, "Finish this bastard off!"

Chago arrived and pulled me away. "Don't do it, Rev. Learn from your dad."

I blinked twice, and my glittering eyes returned to the world around me. I rolled my beaten-up adversary onto his stomach, cuffed him, and said, "You're under arrest."

Chago helped us both to our feet.

The crowd applauded as we walked Boxer to a waiting squad car. A second squad car sped off with the two *vatos* Chago had collared.

"Where to, Sarge?"

"The interrogation room."

A half hour later, Boxer, his face puffy and scratched, held an ice pack to his swollen head. He wore an orange jump suit and sat with his free hand cuffed to a chair, both feet also in chains. He sat across the table from Chago and myself.

Chago turned on a tape recorder. "We're recording our conversation, Boxer, and you have the right to remain silent or ask for an attorney. But this one is between you and Officer Revenir here, between you going to death row, or you spending a few years in the can for assault. Understand?"

Boxer looked down and stayed silent.

I growled. "Why'd you kill Vero, Boxer? What'd she do to you to deserve that?"

"Vero's dead?" Boxer looked at me in disbelief.

"Yeah, and you killed her. I know because I was with her moments before you and your guys got to her apartment. Were you jealous? Did this over-the-top anger of yours kick in one too many times?"

Chago raised an eyebrow and gave me a questioning look.

"I didn't kill her. I came there to kill you and get even for my pop. We had you set up, then she let you off the hook and locked the door, and you got away. I got pissed, and yeah, I did smack her around."

I churned inside with the thought Vero had played me, set me up for a merciless beating. But I also remembered her tears and frantic apology before I escaped.

"Didn't you tell her not to mess with you, or you'd mess her face up so bad men would only like her for her body after that?"

"Yeah, I said that just to scare her. I did slap her hard a couple of times, and I pushed her into a big wall mirror that fell and broke, but we went there hunting for *you*, not her. Ask my homies. They were there. They'll tell you. Vero was hurting, lying on a sofa, but very much alive when we left. You gotta believe that."

Chago pulled no verbal punches. "You beat her up, slashed her throat, ripped her off, and let her bleed out. What kind of animal does that to an unarmed woman?"

Boxer gave him a hard look. "We...I hit her around. I admit it. But we didn't slash her throat or rip her off. We didn't do those things! You got the wrong guys!"

Boxer, head bent, seemed beaten down by his past.

I pressed on. "What'd you do with her necklace and earrings?"

"What're you talking about? We don't know nuthin' about that."

"Did you or your guys take money from her wallet?"

"Hell no. We don't rip off chicks!"

"Any last questions, Boxer?"

"Why didn't you kill me in the street when you had the chance?"

"If we don't learn from our mistakes, their ghosts will come back and hit us hard somewhere up the line. 'Like father, like son' isn't always the right answer. Wasn't the right one for you, and it wasn't right for me."

"You're a prime suspect for murder, Boxer," Chago said. "We'll see if your story holds water when we talk to your buddies."

I shut off the recorder and pushed it over to Chago. Two officers stepped in to escort Boxer to a cell.

"Sarge, we still have one more lead to track down. How about you talking to the parents of Lupe, the roommate? They're probably native Spanish speakers, and you'll have a better chance to locate her whereabouts than me."

Chago found an empty squad room. He closed the door and called Moreno Valley. There, he charmed the socks off Mrs. Ortega. He told her he had three hundred dollars in bonus money for her daughter as a reward for work she had done and wanted to surprise her with it before he left for Vegas tonight. Mrs. Ortega gladly volunteered the information.

After disconnecting, Chago said, "We gotta use subterfuge sometimes, Rev, if we're fighting the clock and have no other alternatives to getting needed answers. This was one of those times. Let's saddle up, partner, we're off to LAX."

British Air Flight #4266 departing at 6 p.m. for Madrid

was on time. Boarding began at five-thirty. Chago called ahead for security clearance. We reached the terminal at just after five.

I spotted Lupe first. "She's wearing Vero's earrings and the Irish pendant. She's the one in a black Raiders sweatshirt seated in the boarding area playing on her phone."

I approached slowly from behind and put my nightstick on the suspect's shoulder. "Get up slowly, Lupe. You're under arrest for the murder of Veronica Lopez. My partner to your right—he'll kill you if you try anything!"

Lupe surrendered without a fight. What could she do, with Chago only ten feet away with his hand on his gun?

Lupe had a Blaq Paq tattoo artist travel bag by her side. In addition to her tat supplies, the carry-on had twenty thousand dollars cash in Benjamins, a bill of sale for a 2016 Explorer, new toiletries, her passport, and a reservation for an apartment in Marbella for an indefinite stay.

At the end of the shift, Chago found Captain Fairchild.

"Cap, I want Rev as my partner from here on."

"After one day? Why?"

"I know gold when I see it. This guy's a keeper. Don't let LAPD sign him."

AUBLE'S GHOST
Julia Bricklin

Frank Chamberlain was a dentist, so the teeth were one of the first things he noticed when he came upon the singed remains. From a distance, he and county surveyor Woodside thought it was a deer or some other animal caught in a bough. When the pair got closer, they could see that it was the body of a young woman. She was white, with long, chestnut-brown hair, which hung down in ringlets frozen by the usual bitter cold of January in Colorado Springs. The body was face down, draped over a long, felled log that was arranged on some rocks and sticks so it was raised about half a foot off the ground. The woman did not have a stitch of clothing on. Chamberlain estimated that she had been rather tall when she was alive—perhaps five-foot, six inches—and no more than thirty years old.

Chamberlain's curiosity got the better of him and he could not help but to gently lift the log to get a look at the victim's face. And there was no doubt about it—she was a victim. There was no other explanation for a young woman to be lying dead, naked and rotting at the foot of Cutler Mountain, far from the center of town. The woman's face was badly disfigured—the top half of it seemed melted away, along with the crown of her hair. Her eyelashes and eyebrows were

173

burned off, and the eyes themselves were so badly burned that it was impossible to tell their color. The teeth, though, were the most interesting. Her back upper teeth were entirely crowned with gold, which, because Chamberlain tilted them upward, caught the afternoon sun and sent dancing rays onto his flannel shirt. They were masterfully formed and planted. This bridgework must have cost a fortune.

The surveyor left Chamberlain to watch the body and got on his horse to go get the sheriff and Coroner Lee. He knew the latter would be really irritated. 1904 had already brought him a year's worth of headaches with mining accidents and labor violence. No doubt he'd want to have some peace going into the Christmas week. Now, he would not get it.

Surveyor Woodside was wrong. Coroner Lee was as clinically amiable as he always was. But Sheriff Grimes was another story. After viewing the body and the .38 caliber slug Lee pulled from the woman's scalp, Grimes knew his vacation time was going to be cut short. Obviously, the woman had been killed, and then the murderer or murderers tried to burn her body by pouring kerosene over it and the logs and took a match to it. He figured a sharp wind gusting down from the mountain had blown the flames out before they could fully take hold.

Grimes dispatched six deputies to search the surrounding area of hills and woods. Over the next four days, the men worked in shifts, three at a time plus some able-bodied volunteers, until they had covered nearly three-square miles. The only items of interest remained those found near the body to begin with: an empty bottle with a bit of kerosene left in it, and a smaller empty bottle with a prescription label bearing the information "Dr. F. K. Linebaker, 3019 Diamond Street, Philadelphia," which turned out to contain a bit of carbolic acid.

First, Coroner Law removed the jaw. Then he snipped off two big locks of her hair. He put these items in a box and allowed Evergreen Cemetery to bury the rest. He wrote a description of the poor woman, as she must have looked like when she was alive, which included her dental work, her clothing, and her height and estimated weight. There were parts of the poor woman that survived the killer's fire, and one of these parts was her left hand, which showed a significant scar—really, still a healing wound—on her left forefinger. Sheriff Grimes gave this description out to anyone who wired him. And many people wired him—there seemed to be no end to the number of people who had not seen loved ones in quite some time.

Eleven hundred miles to the west, Los Angeles Police Captain Walter Hurman Auble read about the dead woman on Cutler Mountain in the *Los Angeles Daily Times*. "Her Teeth May Tell: Dental Work in Mouth of Girl Found Murdered Near Colorado Springs Possible Clew." The paper reported that the metal and labor for the girl's oral cosmetic help was estimated to be worth about a hundred and fifty dollars. Someone with that kind of money, he thought while playing with his long droopy moustache, would surely have family clamoring for news of her soon. Her body would be claimed.

Auble was correct. The dead woman's sister identified her as Bessie Bouton. As well, said sister, Mrs. Charles Nelson of Santa Barbara, confirmed that she had not heard from her sister in some time. Well, Auble thought, good for Colorado Springs. The one Jane Doe it had in years it solved in a week, while the bodies of unnamed souls in Los Angeles's morgue was piled three thick.

The captain was just about to move on to an article about horseracing at the Agriculture Park when a word jumped off the page: "Diamonds." He read more about Bessie Bouton, in the story from up north:

Chief of Santa Barbara police Ross believes that she was murdered by the man who has been living with and traveling with Mrs. Bouton. They visited this city last August together, having come from the East, and were here for a month with Mr. and Mrs. Charles L. Nelson, at No. 1111 State Street. While here Mrs. Bouton displayed a great many very beautiful jewels, mostly diamonds, which her relatives say were valued at over three thousand dollars. She was fond of displaying these jewels and wore them on all occasions.

Auble took a sip of coffee and kept reading. According to the paper, Bouton's companion was one Mr. Milton Franklin Andrews. The paper described him as dark-complexioned, about six feet tall, with a small black moustache, a thin face, high cheekbones, dark brown eyes, and thick, curly brown hair. He was extremely thin—perhaps one hundred fifty pounds at most. Notably, he was pigeon-toed, and also had a slight hunch of the shoulders, giving the impression that his torso was somewhat concave.

Auble's sternum clenched. He would not have thought anything about these two pieces of information separately—the diamonds, and the description of Bouton's male consort—but together, they formed a splotchy image—a familiar feeling of dread in the pit of his stomach. He flashed to a memory. He remembered the woman who lived on West Sixteenth Street, Permelia Bosler, who told him about the strange couple she saw going in and out of the home diagonally across the street from her. The female was attractive, Bosler thought: probably not a natural blonde, but the kind of subtle honey-brown that can be produced by enough money and time in a hairdresser's chair. She was too far away for Bosler to see her complexion and whether there were any blemishes, but she could see that her pallor was translucent and consistent, with a lovely spot of red where her lipsticked mouth was. And she was slim, which she could tell by her waistline, even with what looked to be an ermine wrap over her shoulders. It was the man that drew most of her attention, though. This figure was tall, she said, and dressed in all black, and wore a Prince Albert coat with a felt hat. As well, she thought, he was dark-complexioned, had a rather slim face, and a head of thick brown, curly dark hair.

The detective put his mug down, then went to his filing cabinet and pulled out some newspaper clippings he'd stashed at the bottom a year and a half before. Mrs. Bosler and her daughter were quoted in some of them. The descriptions of Bessie Bouton's lover, Milton Franklin Andrews, reminded him of the man that Mrs. Bosler saw going in and out of 821 West Sixteenth before a real estate agent and his client discovered George Mills' blood-soaked corpse. He forced himself to re-read parts of the *L.A. Times* article about the most depraved and gory act of villainy he had yet encountered on the job:

There was nothing to indicate that there had been the slightest struggle of any kind. The legs were straight, the hands were clenched and the cuffs about both wrists were bloody although as the body lay it was impossible that they could have reached the bloody floor. The bed nearby was as it had been left, the coverings not being disturbed in the least and even the rug on which the body lay was in its usual position.

Auble tried not to gag as he recalled the smell, conjured by the words in the paper. As a seasoned cop, it took even him by surprise:

Lying on his face in a pool of blood was the body of a man. His hands were bound behind his back with a piece of sash cord, which was also tightly bound around his neck, several knots being tied in the rope. The head was a mass of putrid flesh, for there was hardly a portion of the scalp which was not cut through to the skull. The rug on which the body was lying was saturated with blood, and blood was spattered on the wall and baseboard.

Notably, the murderer—or murderers—had removed a giant diamond stud from Mills's necktie. They also took what little cash he had in his pockets. But later, when detectives queried his wife at the Mills's home, she led them into his study where she nearly fainted, pointing to the open safe. "He had about ten thousand dollars' worth of diamonds in there," she said. Wasn't it rather unusual to keep such an enormous number of gems, Auble and his men had asked her. Not at all, she said, because he was a manager for the Syndicate Loan Company, which was a fancy term for "pawnbroker," she added. Mills often purchased expensive furniture for well-heeled clients who paid him in gems or jewelry.

Auble pulled on his coat and shut the door to his office on South Hope Street. He brushed aside the young rank-and-file who tried to get his attention. He needed to wire Chief Reynolds in Colorado City for some photographs.

He got the photographs and sketches a week later. The images were, as he'd imagined, gruesome. Were it not for the note Reynolds had placed on top of the sketches, he might have missed the treasure enclosed underneath them, wrapped carefully in brown butcher's paper: a small grove of hair strands glued to a piece of cardboard. *Captain Auble*, the note read, *Herewith a sample of hair from the deceased, Bessie Bouton, in the event it can serve you to find whomever may be a monster shared by our cities.*

Auble tapped a young patrolman to drive him from police headquarters at 1817 South Hope Street to 840 West Sixteenth Street. As he pulled up, he could see Mrs. Bosler standing on a crate in her front yard, pruning a fig tree. Her daughter, pulling weeds nearby, heard him first and tugged on her mother's skirt. Bosler got down, straightened up and brushed her skirt. "What can I do for you, Captain Auble?" The officer gestured toward the front of her home. "Okay if we go inside?"

Auble spared Mrs. Bosler the sight of the photographs of the Cutler Mountain corpse. Instead, he showed her only the strands of hair that Sheriff Grimes had taped to the piece of cardboard, and the sketches that Coroner Law drew of what he thought the dead woman might have looked like when she was alive and well. Could she be the woman Permelia saw luring Mills into the home across the street? The woman wiped her brow as she looked at these items. December in Los Angeles might as well be late spring anywhere else. "That's her, alright," the matron swore.

The detective thanked her and left. He walked across the street and stared at the house where George Mills was slaughtered. It was a pretty, mint-green, two-story cottage of eight rooms, and stood by itself on the north side of the street. Green lawns and dots of geranium beds surrounded it. A wealthy harness maker and his wife owned the house. It had, for obvious reasons, remained vacant since Mills was killed twenty months ago. Auble felt sorry for the owners. No doubt they would have a hard time renting it out again after what happened there, he thought.

At age forty-four, Auble thought he had seen enough depravity and violence for ten lifetimes. Born in Illinois and raised in Savannah, Missouri, he moved to Southern California in 1887 and got a job with LAPD almost immediately. A day after he put on his badge, he had to rescue a Chinese toddler from fire at a hovel on Sanchez Street. Hardly a day went by without breaking up a fan-tan ring, an opium den, a house of prostitution, drunken mothers and fathers, a burglary outfit. The first man he actually shot was William Bean, whom he had seen jimmying a lock at Joe Ludwig's fruit store on Temple and Hill. Auble shot him after yelling at him to stop running away. The bullet entered Bean's spine at such an angle that the receiving hospital doctor said he would die within a day. He did not, and instead, took Auble to court and accused the detective of entrapping him. Why else would an officer of such stature happen to be watching the back of a fruit store from a room across the street at eleven-thirty at night?

Auble was acquitted, as usual. But the press dubbed Bean "Auble's ghost," and the inference was clear: the detective had spent so much time with low-level thugs that maybe he was becoming callous and sloppy and tired, and maybe he had taken some liberties with the truth of what happened. It didn't help that once the patient woke up, Bean's handwritten "deathbed confession" exonerating Auble was proved to be bogus. Walter knew it was time to move on to more intellectual pursuits within the department. He'd earned it. His chief would not be retiring any time soon, but he did put Auble in charge of only big crimes. The only criminals this strapping Midwestern lawman would handle were big ones: highway robbers, large-scale bunco-steerers, and murderers. This was a big one, this Mills murder. He needed to solve it.

"'Member that Pinkerton bullshit?" asked the eager young patrolman when Auble climbed back into the motorcar. He'd decided to go on home since it was getting late, and his house was on the Sixteenth Street route as well, albeit a few miles east. He didn't answer the younger man, but of course he remembered the Pinkerton bullshit. At two o'clock in the morning the day after George Mills' body was discovered, that smarmy bastard from the San Francisco office sashayed into 821 Sixteenth Street, spilling hot coffee all over the foyer. "You," said the interloper, nodding at one of Auble's men, "have a go at that with a rag, will you, son?" The young cop stared bug-eyed at Charles Ryan's shield, glinting in the electric lights of the house. Auble stepped between his charge and Ryan.

"This is a homicide scene," he growled. "What's your business here?"

"Maybe you didn't see the shield, son," the man said, "I'm with Pinkerton's. Using Sheriff Biscailuz's office until Ascot Park opens."

"Means as much to me as a fart in a whirlwind," Auble said. "Do what you have to do and get out. And clean up your own goddamned coffee."

The Pinkerton detective made a big show of looking into corners of the house and lifting up papers here and there, muttering "Uh, uh hm," every thirty seconds. After about fifteen minutes of this, the man cried, "A-ha!" so loudly that Auble dropped his own coffee. The uninvited private eye waved a little piece of cardboard. It was a baggage check from a Tucson hotel. "I will no doubt discern," said the Pinkerton, "that whomever this baggage check belonged to is our killer!"

Auble had a feeling that no killer would be stupid enough to leave such evidence behind. He was right; the claim check could not be matched to anyone who had stayed at that hotel in recent years. But the clue did serve one good purpose, and that was to get Pinkerton's off on a wild goose chase and out of the hair of LAPD for a couple of months. And Detective Ryan was so excited about this inconsequential piece of paper that he completely missed what Auble did not: the nest of bizarre food products in the kitchen—a fresh bag of malted milk powder, a jar of nut butter, and a can of "Protose Meat Substitute," all made by Battle Creek Sanitarium. Auble knew that the man who butchered George Mills was a monster who, in his brain, might be soothed by acting upon his murderous impulses, but whose bowels buckled under the stress of being attached to an abomination of nature.

The next day, Auble rapped on the door of his boss, Chief Hammell. "Remember the Sixteenth Street case?" he asked, feeling confident enough to spread out papers and photographs on the Chief's desk. Hammell did remember it. He just didn't care much about it. "I still believe that it was a lover's quarrel," he said dismissively. "Probably even a coupla Sallys. The woman was probably a sister or a maid or even a figment of the neighbor's imagination," he said.

Auble sucked in his breath. Sometimes he could not believe the man sitting in the chair in front of him was chief of all Los Angeles police. He plowed ahead. "I believe the murderer of George Mills is the same man who killed this poor thing in

Colorado City. The man and woman seen at 821 Sixteenth match the description of Andrews and Bouton, and there were diamonds stolen from both Mills and Bouton."

"There are a lot of 'tall and dark' men who would kill for a quantity of diamonds," Hammell responded with a yawn.

"But not in such a depraved way," Auble said. "This killer is taking a great deal of risk and effort to obliterate the very image of his victims once he has acquired their gems. He doesn't even bother taking cash and other valuables." He thought for a beat, and then said, "He is not going to stop. He can't stop. I think he's been here before, and he will strike again in Los Angeles."

"Captain." Hammell sighed. "I know how badly you want that big one." Auble thought it was quaint that Hammell, born in Los Angeles, still accented some words the way his German parents did. "That big one" sounded like "Dat big wan." But his point was taken. Auble did want this mad man. He should have been able to track him down in 1903. Maybe he could have saved the life of poor Bessie Bouton, stripped of her humanity on Cutler Mountain.

"Chief," said Auble. "Do you remember when I was asked to send some of my men and a medical expert to San Pedro last September?" Hammell nodded and checked his watch. "The woman who got off the ferry boat from Santa Catalina was so sick she was foaming at the mouth and bleeding from...well, she was bleeding from everywhere she should not. She barely survived." Hammell nodded even more vigorously and gestured for Auble to hurry up. "The woman," the captain continued, "looked just like this one, and the nurses reported that she kept clutching the fingers of her left hand. When they pried them open, her left forefinger was cut deep, right below the diamond solitaire ring there. The gem turned out to be almost four carats."

"So, she was a rich one," Hammell said. "So, what?"

"So," Auble continued, "at first, the doctor assumed that

the cut was because her limbs were entirely swollen because her kidneys were trying like hell to get the poison out, and that the band cut into her finger. But later, he realized that, in fact, someone had tried to cut off her finger at the base with a dull knife…but it didn't work. Or more likely, the other passengers heard her screaming before the villain could finish the deed."

"Right," Hammell said. "So, the criminal wanted to get the diamond off her before her body was found. Seems like a natural thing for a killer to take, after going through dat much trouble. Probably what he was after all along, a gem that big."

"Yes," Auble said, "look here at the Colorado Springs coroner's description of Bessie Bouton's corpse. 'Fresh scar on left forefinger.' Bessie's sister identified her body by her dental work. But there was also the wound on her hand. Yesterday, I telephoned Mrs. Nelson, her sister. She confirmed that she and her husband had vacationed with Bessie and her fiancée in Los Angeles last August. The Nelsons returned to Santa Barbara late in the month, while Bessie and her beau were headed to Catalina and then to Colorado. She never heard from her sister again."

"Alright, then. So, who was the beau?" asked Hammell.

"One Milton Franklin Andrews, from Mount Holyoke, Massachusetts," Auble said, pounding Hammell's table. "And according to the Nelsons, Bessie was absolutely besotted with this man. He tried hard to put on a polite face when they were around, but oftentimes, late in the day, he lost control, thinking she was looking at other men. He would yell at her and threaten to take away all of her belongings and her engagement ring. A regular Jekyll and Hyde, according to the Nelsons. After a nap or a meal, Franklin would apologize profusely, and give Bessie a tiny little diamond or two, and claim that he was just looking out for her best interests."

"Okay, so what does all of this have to do with a murderer who may or may not still be on the loose in Los Angeles?"

Hammell asked.

"Besides Franklin's unpleasant nature," Auble continued, "the Nelsons said they could not vacation with the pair any longer, because they could not dine out with the other couple. Franklin required very specialized foods, including large quantities of malted milk and odd, prepackaged food. They often had to spend half the day looking for stores that carried products from Battle Creek Sanitarium."

Finally, Chief Hammell understood. "All right, so the man who killed Mills on Sixteenth Street is the same man who killed his lover in Colorado Springs. Why do we think that he would come back here?"

Three reasons, Auble explained. The first was obvious: Los Angeles was an itinerant town. One could hop off a steamship in Long Beach or a train at Grand Central, and immediately get lost in anonymity. Even in 1905, you could pretend you were anybody, from anywhere, even if you weren't. Second, he said, was related to the first. There were simply a lot more people who could be a "mark." Well-to-do people who liked to flaunt diamonds and live vicariously at gambling dens and stay at hotels among strangers were more likely to be found in Los Angeles or San Francisco or New York than they were in—say—Iowa City. And frankly, Los Angeles had the best weather.

The third reason was the most important, and Auble "thump thumped" on the pertinent newspaper article on Hammell's desk: "Glendale to Open Largest Battle Creek Sanitarium on Pacific Coast," said the *Los Angeles Beacon*. It was dated August 5, 1904. Auble pushed several smaller articles from area papers since then, noting the progress of this "health hotel" just north of the city, in the dry junction of the San Gabriel and San Fernando valleys. It would, added the stories, be the largest distributor of its famous foods for temperamental digestive systems. "There is no question," Auble said, "that Franklin went to Colorado Springs so he could isolate Bouton from her sister. Remember, he thought her body would be unidentifiable from the fire. He will have no choice but to hide in a large city, and we know he has come to Los Angeles at least twice and feels comfortable here. And he will not be able to shake his need for diamonds and predigested Zwieback toast or whatever the hell it is that he eats."

Hammell turned his nose at this last comment and then chuckled. "Okay, I'm convinced. What would you like to do? Need men? Money?"

Auble thought for a moment. "No. I don't need 'em. Just an extra secretary for a day."

The next day, the captain telegraphed the harbor masters in San Pedro, Long Beach, and Los Angeles, warning them to be on the lookout for a man fitting Franklin's odd description. Most likely, Auble noted, he would be traveling with an attractive, blonde companion, as was his usual preference. The detective also telegraphed all the major railroad depots between San Diego and San Luis Obispo counties to be on the lookout.

Nothing. For seven long months, nothing. In his spare time (scant with four children at home), Auble followed up with victims of jewelry heists, women who had been beaten by their husbands or lovers, and health food stores that sold Battle Creek goods, hoping to find the name of someone who placed any large or regular orders (there were literally hundreds—too many to interview). He trolled gambling dens in his regular clothes, looking for anyone who was using diamonds, either as collateral or accepting them as a substitute for cash winnings. As the weeks turned into months and summer turned from pleasantly hot in June to blistering hot in August, Auble found himself increasingly irritated by his on—the—clock responsibilities, busting "blind pigs" and illegal faro games and liberating women in "disorderly places." But being a captain with the LAPD comes with some perks, and one of them was being sent to the cool, mild shores of Avalon, Santa Catalina with thirteen of your most athletic patrolmen to play baseball against San Francisco's fourteen most crack men in blue—which is what happened on July 12, 1905.

San Francisco's team routed Auble's team, but nobody minded. The constable of the island invited both teams to inspect his new jail, and when all of the bluecoats were looking at the Spanish-style wainscoting, he playfully shut the barred door and captured his "prisoners." While all the junior officers enjoyed the beer, dinner and party given them in their "cell," Auble took aside his old friend, Jeremiah Dinan, Captain of the San Francisco Police Department. He explained the history of the Andrews specter, and promised to have his secretary send all the information and theories he held for the lethal figure in fashionable clothing. Peterson shrugged at the story—his city had its own share of peculiar evildoers—but he promised to put out a bulletin when he returned home. "I'll be sure to alert Marshal Vollmer, too," Dinan said, referring to the new lawman in Berkeley. "Malted milk? Are you sure?"

The next day, before getting on the steamship Cabrillo with his tired but happy men to go home, Auble had a private word with their host, Avalon's Constable Allen. Of course, Allen remembered Bessie Bouton and her consort from the summer before. How could he forget? He had queried the druggist on the island right after he read about Bessie almost dying upon reaching San Pedro. He had sold carbolic acid to a man fitting Franklin's description just two days before Bouton returned to the mainland, riddled with poison.

Exactly two months later, on October 12, 1905, Florence Auble answered the call from the Central girl, who relayed Captain Dinan through to her husband. Walter Auble was now acting chief, owing to Hammell's resignation in late August. Mrs. Auble liked it when the operator said, "Chief Auble," but she knew her husband was not thrilled at political nonsense that came with the job—it was the reason Hammell quit.

"Auble," Dinan said excitedly. "There's been a big development. I believe your ghost man is here!" The acting chief could barely contain himself and strained to hear more against the static piped through the instrument. He explained that an Australian man, one William Ellis, showed up at Roosevelt Hospital in Oakland, with severe head wounds. The man—a wealthy horse breeder—had arrived in the States a few days earlier with a couple who had befriended him back in Australia. The man and woman were inveterate gamblers, as was he. The couple had talked Ellis into going to Honolulu with them, to play in a tournament. The male lured Ellis to a picturesque but remote piece of land there called Diamond Head, and the next thing he knew, a bullet whizzed past his ear!

"'Diamond Head.' You're not serious, man. Are you?"

"Dreadfully serious," Dinan responded.

"Why on Earth didn't this gentleman flee for his life?" Auble said.

"Well," Dinan continued, "Ellis is wealthy, but he is dumber than a double-clamped oyster. Believed the fella when he said the gun discharged accidentally. And speaking of shells, this guy's skull was smashed so hard it's a miracle he is alive, never mind able to talk."

"I don't understand. If he wasn't shot, why is he in one of your hospitals?"

Dinan relayed the whole story. Ellis simply could not resist the charms of this would-be assassin, and even loaned him substantial sums of money to gamble with. "Even though I detested the man—" Dinan read Ellis's statement off his notes, "—and tried to keep away from him, when I met him face to face I forgot his wrongdoings and could not help liking him." So much so, he explained, that Ellis agreed to sail to California with him and the blonde that was his wife. At least, she was supposed to be his wife. They would bet on the horse track in Emeryville, and then head down to Ascot Park if their winnings got too big or too small.

Exasperated, Auble urged him to continue.

"I had your rather fantastical description of the man observed going in and out of that Los Angeles home in 1903— the one who murdered your banker fellow?" Dinan said. "Every copper up here knew about him, though I have to admit, we all thought you might be having us looking for a phantom." Auble rolled his eyes and let the captain continue, so he wouldn't get distracted. "Well, O'Brien got a ring from a Mrs. Hornbeck, who owns a little grocery and bakery at number 743 McAllister Street. There was this young woman who came into her store daily to buy large amounts of Battle Creek malted milk, and a dozen eggs at a time. She always kept her head down and spoke rather softly, and would never make the usual talk about family, where she was from, and so forth. Well, one day last week, this gal shows up with bleachedblonde hair, and wearing smoked glasses. Mrs. Hornbeck had not been following the Ellis story in the papers, so she figured this woman had merely fallen into idiocy. But when her son mentioned the story over dinner that evening and talked about the strange couple that came to town with Ellis, she formed the opinion that this woman could be Franklin's latest paramour."

"Yes! And?" Auble said.

"We thought she was batty and paid her no mind," Dinan said. "We get these kinds of old ladies all the time, trying to be 'part of the action,' you know. We had most of our men at the Ellsworth Street cottage where Ellis says he was bludgeoned by a hammer from behind. We busted open the cottage and found the most terrible sight you ever saw: oil cloths laid out on the floor; a bowie knife, a stiletto, and a butcher knife, all laid out on a dining table. We found a bottle of carbolic acid and rubber gloves hidden under a mattress. Clearly, this pair planned to dispose of Ellis's body."

"Was any money taken from Ellis?" Auble asked.

"Nearly one thousand British pounds and a pair of diamond

cufflinks," Dinan said. "Remarkably, Ellis was able to fend off more blows even after being hit from behind. His right forearm is broken, but it's a miracle he is not dead. The doctors say he has a skull at least twice the thickness of an ordinary man. I'm inclined to believe them." Dinan chuckled at his observation. "Point is, we showed him your sketches of your Sixteenth Street man, and those of the man who killed Bessie Bouton. They are one in the same, and Ellis says they are definitely the man he knows as William Brush...real name Milton Franklin Andrews."

"What about the woman at the health food store?" Auble asked, excited.

"Yes, well. We are going to follow her the next time she comes in. Although, given what has happened, she—if it is she—and this Andrews terror might be long gone."

"They're not gone," Auble said. "They're holed up somewhere, trying to figure out how to get another roll of cash to leave the country. Keep an eye on poker games, the race track, and this blonde at the grocery," he said. "I'm going to be on the next train to Oakland. I'll meet with you and Vollmer there."

Acting Chief Walter Auble arrived in Oakland on October 14th. He visited the Australian, who was recuperating at his hotel, and quickly realized this victim was quickly cashing in on his newfound celebrity. Auble had to shoo away several young women and one young man who had gathered around to offer financial support in return for the pleasure of Ellis's company. The chief interviewed the former jockey about Andrews's current female companion.

"She first told me her name was Julia Ward," Ellis said. "But I overheard Brush—er, Andrews—call her 'Nulda' one night, and she confided that that was her real name, Nulda Petrie Oliva. Odd name, eh? Canadian. She is lovely. I should say, she was lovely until she tried to kill me."

Florence Auble was upset when her husband telephoned her the evening of October 15th. He would not be coming home until he caught or killed Milton Franklin Andrews, even if he had to stay in San Francisco until Christmas. He didn't care if the mayor did not give him the permanent chief job. In fact, he hoped he wouldn't. It might even be time to move his family back to the Midwest. Or better, some farm land up in Oregon.

As it turned out, he did not have to stay in the Bay Area for very long. On November 6th, at his usual perch at the café across the street from Mrs. Hornbeck's healthful grocery, Auble watched as a platinum blonde barely constrained by a scarf looked both ways over her shoulders and walked into the store. It was dusk, but there was no mistaking that it was the woman who could be—was likely—Franklin's latest companion. He waited until she left with her bags of boxed food, and slipped behind her, careful not to get too close or to make his footsteps too loud. Auble knew that he, too, was being followed. He stole a furtive glance behind him as he rounded Octavia Street and immediately recognized two of Dinan's detectives. That was fine. He hoped they would play it safe.

The blonde woman climbed the steps at 748 McAllister. She looked around again before unlocking and pushing in the front door, straining with her groceries. Auble waited for a few minutes. No one else came in or out of the home. He crept around the side of the structure, scraping himself against the thorned bushes, hoping no neighbors would see him and scream. He peered through the lace curtains of what seemed to be a living room window. On the floor, he could see suitcases. Looking more to the right, he saw a massive maple table with all manner of coats and dresses and several brown bottles of liquid. The setting sun captured a glint of something that made Auble wince and pull back a little. He rubbed his eye and looked again: there was a brand-new ax lying next to a pair of sunglasses. He knew in his gut that this was Nulda's last night on Earth.

Auble crept further along the house toward the back yard, waiting for a car to pass before cocking his pistol as quietly as he could. Just as he reached the back door, he heard a loud splintering of wood. A crash. Voices yelling. "POLICE! PUT 'EM UP! PUT 'EM UP!" Two shots!

"It's him! It's him! You were right!" San Francisco Detective Freel yelled at Auble, who had rushed into the room. The woman, no doubt Nulda, lay in almost perfect repose on a cot in the corner of the living room and her hands clasped in front of her, with her fingers interlocked. Blood oozed from a wound in her left temple and was splattered all over the walls. Andrews's self-inflicted bullet had entered his right temple. His left hand, which had clasped his .44 caliber, lay still next to his crumpled body at the base of the cot. He'd shot his lover, and then himself.

Auble was made permanent Chief of LAPD on November 20, 1905. Florence convinced him that a few years of political nonsense would be a small price to pay for a large salary and a safe job behind a desk. Sometimes, when it looked to his employees like he was reading the latest crime reports, Auble would re-read the many letters he copied from those found in the McCallister house. Andrews had confessed not only to Bessie Bouton's murder, but several others across the country. He asked that if he was caught or killed that the police and newspapers take mercy on his wife in Mount Holyoke, who knew nothing about his activities and thought he was just a traveling salesman. Andrews's rage could be seen to ebb and flow even in his writings, which vacillated between apologies and indictments: "If I had known Ellis had the skull of a gorilla," he wrote, "I would have hired a pile driver."

On Thanksgiving Day, 1905, Auble took his youngest child for an outing in his department-issued electric car. They drove to 821 Sixteenth Street. It was rented. Auble smiled.

RESURRECTION
Jennifer Younger

Jimmy Pritchard lit his last cigarette in an alley near 42nd and Central Avenue. He could hear the end of "Washerwoman Blues" being sung by some nobody singer coming from Club Alabam a few doors down. Jazz. Swing. Bebop. Blues. He always found his way back to this part of town because this was where the good music was. Besides colored dudes always had something going down, so maybe he could score.

He looked at the date of the Los Angeles Sentinel that he had picked up out of the garbage. Saturday, March 20, 1948. He was two weeks and two days out from an eighteen-month stretch in the joint for burglary. It should have been less time, but he mouthed off to the judge. Now he was out and just wanted to breathe in clean, fresh air.

Jimmy leaned against the brick wall savoring every bit of the harsh, bitter tobacco scorching the back of his throat. His mouth was dry for the taste of whiskey. He needed money, but he wasn't going back to the joint by getting caught doing whatever he was going to do. He'd have to figure out a smarter way to fill his wallet. Take that big score in '36. He'd got paid all right, only because he didn't tell Big Ed that the girl was dead. Didn't nobody still know what happened to her. He didn't mean for her to end up dead, sometimes shit just goes sideways. But that was a long time ago, and he had learned a lot over the years as a career thug.

Hessie Mae was not a pretty woman. She was prematurely gray and her right eye drooped just enough to be noticeable. She looked closer to fifty than the actual twenty-seven that she was. And then there was the way she walked, her hips swaying back and forth to the rhythm of music that only she could hear. Sashaying right and left like she was putting on a show, but that was the only way she could walk.

The sounds of a shovel hitting hard dirt and clinking against sharp rock whispered in her left ear. Although the thing happened twelve years ago, nothing stopped the sound. Not the melting ice tinkling in a half-full glass of liquor. Not the blare of the jukebox or the banging of pots and pans from the dishwashers inside the restaurant where she worked.

Absently, Hessie flicked at her earlobe, trying to brush the sound away, but it stayed. A shovel hitting dirt; a shovel hitting rock. Always in her ear. The empty grave she crawled out of a shadow in the corner of her eye.

She emptied a bucket of scraps and peels from the kitchen into the garbage bins outside. Glancing down the alley, she noticed a white man walking toward her. He looked familiar. His shape. His height.

Hessie took the Chesterfield cigarettes she had stuffed in her bra and pulled one out of the pack. The striking of the match lit up part of the alley. She lifted her eyes just a little. He was coming closer.

"Hey! Got one of those for me?" he asked as he approached. His sharp tone startled her.

She looked him over. Straggly blond hair, jail workhouse dungarees, and old army coat. Hessie wondered what this white dude was doing in the neighborhood.

Club Alabam. Must be. It was either the jazz that drew him here or he was a pimp. Must be the music. No pimps would be looking to set her out on the stroll. She kept her head down as he walked closer.

Hessie took a long drag of her cigarette and let the smoke out slowly. She looked up and watched as his face came into view in the dim light.

"Hey, I asked you for a smoke."

She stared into his eyes and threw up at his feet.

"Wha the fu—?" he screamed while shaking the puke off his boot.

Hessie threw the pack of cigarettes at him, her hand shaking as she ran back into the diner's kitchen. She almost tore the screen door off its hinges. She didn't stop running until she reached the women's restroom, which was for customers only. Slamming the door behind her, Hessie rested the side of her face against the cool tiles that covered the walls and tried to catch her breath. She cursed at her shock and fear.

"Shit! Shit! Shit!" She hurried into the stall and threw up again.

A few minutes later, she emerged and walked over to one of the sinks. She bathed her face in cool water and washed out her mouth.

Hessie had recognized him instantly. It was his eyes, his beautiful crystal blue eyes. Twelve years, but she couldn't forget those eyes. She clawed at her left ear. Shovel hitting hard dirt, clinking against sharp rock. That hideous laugh. The unbearable pain.

"Hessie! Hester Mae?" Ruth Ann's stern voice brought Hessie out of her nearly unresponsive state.

"Girl, what's wrong? Ruth Ann asked.

Hessie blinked in confusion. "I'm alright."

"Well, you don't look right." The concern still in her voice.

"I said I'm fine Ruth Ann. Let me be." Hessie turned away from her friend and went back to work.

＊ ＊ ＊

A few nights later, Hessie saw Jimmy come strolling down the alley. He was back.

"Gotta smoke? Jimmy asked.

Hessie stood still, the scraps bucket dangled from her fingers. Absently, she clawed at her left ear. Her eyes grew wide as he stepped closer.

She swallowed hard, willing herself not to throw up again. The shock of Jimmy showing up in her life after all this time made her chest hurt. Hessie set the bucket down and lit a cigarette. Except for his eyes, time had not been good to him.

Tapping another one out of the pack, she handed it to him. Her fingers sizzled as they touched his.

Hessie could see he had no idea who she was.

Well, she would make him remember. She'd make him remember all the things she could never forget.

Jimmy nodded toward the restaurant. "You know if they got any work here?"

"Ruth Ann don't hire no ex-cons." Hessie's hand shook as she lit the cigarette she tapped out for herself.

"Why you think I'm an ex-con?"

"Them jailhouse dungarees, ain't they?" She pitched the half-smoked cigarette in the small puddle of water.

"How long you work here?" he asked.

"Long time. Long time." She was deliberate with each word. The hate Hessie felt for him festered in her breast. She looked into his eyes, and the anger grew. She grabbed the empty bucket and turned to go back inside.

"Say, don't you want to have a smoke?"

"Why you keep comin' around here?" she asked. "I ain't got nuthin for ya."

"Say, girl, lemme ask you something. You know where a guy could, you know, score a—?"

Hessie stopped and looked down at him from the top step.

"No." She opened the screen door and stepped inside.

"I don't mean dope!" Jimmy said in a loud whisper. "Look, I mean I could really use some cash. I need a job. I'll do anything."

"I'll see." She closed and locked the screen door, then called out to Ruth Ann on her way went back into the kitchen.

Ruth Ann came up beside Hessie as she washed dishes.

"I need you to do something for me," Hessie whispered.

"What?"

"You know that dude Jimmy that comes around the alley at night? I need you to give him a job."

"You mean that white boy you been hangin' out wit? Why you messin' with him?"

"He's an ex-con, Ruth Ann. I just need you to do this for me."

"What's this about, Hessie? You know I don't need no trouble with ex-cons 'round here."

Hessie reached down, picked up another bucket of scraps and headed outside to the garbage cans. She could feel Ruth Ann behind her as she emptied the scrap bucket.

"He's just someone to smoke with." Hessie paused to light up a cigarette. "He likes the music down there at the Alabam. He comes by and grabs a smoke off me." Hessie sucked in a lungful, blowing out blue-grey smoke that floated up and circled around the single dim light bulb at the back door.

"Well you bess be careful. He don't look too right ta me."

Hessie drew on her cigarette and held in the smoke. "Ever notice how beautiful the sky is? Look at that moon."

"Girl, you crazy, whatcho talkin' about? The sky and the moon?" Ruth Ann walked down the steps and stood next to Hessie. The slight breeze felt nice. The kitchen inside was too hot, too small, and crammed in too many people. Ruth Ann seemed grateful to sneak away for a little break.

Hessie leaned against the wall, staring down at the cigarette in her hand. She was quiet for a long time. Absently she pulled at her left ear.

"We been tight a long time, right?" Ruth Ann said. "Let me ask you tho'. Why you always do that? Scratch at your ear like that?"

"You really want to know? Hessie hesitated. "It's rough. Maybe you won't want to like me no more after you hear the whole story."

Ruth Ann lightly touched her shoulder. "Can't nothing you say gonna worry me."

"I was kidnapped and raped when I was fifteen. Left for dead." Hessie was surprised at how easily the words tumbled out.

"Law'd...Merciful Jesus! You mean that girl they said was buried up in the hills? You mean that?"

"Yeah. But the grave wasn't deep enough. I held my breath and kept still. Jimmy, that bastard I been seein' in the alley, he's the one that did it to me. Rolled me in a hole he dug and threw dirt on me. He thought I was dead."

Ruth Ann and Hessie were quiet. Both leaned against the brick wall in the alley. It was a long time before Hessie spoke again.

"Junior got into some shit with Big Ed."

"Junior? Your brother Junior?" Ruth Ann raised her brow, and then nodded her head. "That boy never been no good. Still no good to this day. I bet he owed somebody money, uh-huh. Sure as I'm standing, he owed somebody money, right? Boy always down on Waverly in one of them jukes gamblin' away his paycheck and anybody else's money he can get his hands on."

Ruth Ann paused and eyed her friend. Her silence prompted Hessie to continue and Hessie's voice shook as she finally let out the whole story. "Big Ed said Junior owed him money and Junior said he didn't owe shit. Dared Big Ed to do something about it. Everyone in the neighborhood knew about Big Ed, who would shoot you in the kneecap or pop one in your ass just for fun. But when Big Ed really wanted to get your attention, he would target your family. Mother. Sister. Wife. Daughter. Only the women, cause that's who you was supposed to protect, right? Jimmy Pritchard was sent to kidnap and hold for ransom Junior's sister. Big Ed said he'd pay Jimmy two thousand dollars to snatch the bitch and hold her until he got his ten large. Should have been easy. Kidnap the girl, hold her out in the woods, wait until morning, and bring her back. That's what Big Ed said."

Hessie stared at her feet. "Next thing I remember, I was in the trunk of a car. I couldn't breathe too good. My hands and my feet were tied behind me and my mouth was taped shut. Ruth Ann, I was scared. I knew I was gonna die." Her chest heaved and even now Hessie had trouble catching her breath.

"But you didn't die, baby. You here. You done saved yourself."

Hessie clawed at her ear again.

"He took me way out in the woods. Up near that place where all the colored folks go in the summertime."

"Val Verde."

"Yeah, that's the place. I think he was supposed to leave me there or something. But then Jimmy got other ideas. He... He did that thing I said before, and almost killed me."

Hessie fell silent again. She lit another cigarette, holding the smoke deep in her lungs before exhaling. "You know what he did after, Ruth Ann? You want to know what he did?"

Ruth Ann stood silent. Waiting.

"He dug a grave. A grave for me! I tried to escape but he caught me and threw me to the ground. He crashed his boot down so hard that he broke my hip. I didn't cry though. I didn't make a single sound. He thought I was dead." Hessie stared at the lit end of her cigarette. "Jimmy didn't dig deep enough. There wasn't enough dirt to cover me. When he left, I held my breath for as long as I could in case he came back." Tears trickled down her face. "He hurt me so bad, Ruth Ann.

I was so scared."

She wiped her eyes with the back of her hand and took another deep drag of her cigarette.

"If it's him, then why...?" Ruth Ann stopped herself. "Is that why you been spendin' all this time out here wit him? Smokin'. Talkin' wit him?"

"I think it is Jimmy's time to die." Hessie exhaled and met Ruth Ann's eyes. "Because a day doesn't go by that I don't hear the sounds of him diggin' that grave for me."

Ruth Ann studied her. Understood. "How you gonna do it?"

No hesitation. No shock. Hessie felt relief. Ruth Ann knew Hessie was gonna to commit cold-blooded murder and she was all right with it.

"I'll need the truck." Hessie said.

"You want me to ride wit you?"

The crackle of cigarette paper and tobacco hung in the air. Hessie clawed at her left ear.

"When?" Ruth Ann said softly.

Hessie flicked the cigarette butt, and it landed it in a small water puddle near the garbage cans. She pulled out another and lit up. "Ask if you can borrow your dad's truck for a few days and leave it at your house. Put the key under the front seat."

"Yeah, I can do that. You know I will help you do this."

"No. You don't know anything. Got it?"

"You lookin' for a better line of work?" Hessie asked Jimmy.

He had been meeting her out in the alley several times during the past week, always looking for a handout smoke. Fucker now worked at the restaurant as a busboy but he was too cheap to buy his own smokes.

"Well, are you?" She forced a smile. "'Cause I got a friend who needs someone to ride with him. Pays good, too. I think he said about a thousand."

"A thousand?" Jimmy asked. "Well shit, why don't you do it?"

"He don't want no woman, he wants a man."

"What's in it for you?"

"I already got my piece, just for asking around. Look, if you don't want to do it, I can find someone else."

"Where and when?"

"Meet me here. Two a.m."

"Two in the morning? Why that time?"

Hessie could almost see those little hairs standing up on the back of Jimmy's neck. He needed the money. She could see he wanted that money.

"Man," she pretended to warn him, "you gonna be in a colored neighborhood, doing something that may not quite be legal. Do you want to do it?"

She saw the greed in his crystal blue eyes.

"I'll be back at two," Jimmy told her.

Two a.m. There he was, right on time.

Hessie was behind the wheel of the truck, motor running. Jimmy opened the passenger side door and got in.

"Where we going?" he asked.

"Not too far."

"Gotta smoke?"

In answer, Hessie pulled out her cigarettes and handed him the pack. He pulled out two and stuck one behind his ear. He then tossed the pack on the seat.

Hessie turned toward the newly constructed interstate. Jimmy didn't seem to notice that they were headed out of town. He just kept puffing away, and rattled on about some stupid jazz band or singer or something. She didn't pay attention to him. She had to concentrate.

They'd been driving for about an hour when she turned

west onto a two-lane highway. The Angeles National Forest was all around them. Another thirty minutes passed, and Hessie turned onto a dirt road. Tools in the bed of the pickup clanged and slid from one side to the other.

"Hey," Jimmy asked in concern, "where we going? You sure you know where we're going? You could whack somebody, and no one would hear!" He laughed.

Hessie said nothing. Focused, she drove over the bumps and divots in the road. Finally, she came to a stop.

"Come on," she told Jimmy as she got out and walked around to the back of the truck. Reaching under the tarp, Hessie pulled out the Winchester pump she had strapped to the inside of the truck bed. Jimmy walked ahead, blinded by the thought of money. Hessie knew he could almost taste it.

He stopped when he heard her ratchet the gun. He didn't move. Didn't turn around.

"Wha...what's going on here, girl? What are we doing out here?"

"Here is where it was, Jimmy. Don't tell me you forgot. Isn't this where you dumped that colored girl twelve years ago?"

"I don't know what...what's going on here." The smell of urine hit the air as Jimmy peed himself. "I don't know what you're talking about. You are the only colored girl I know. I didn't know nobody like that twelve years ago. Shit, I wasn't even in Los Angeles in November of '36!"

"Sure know a lot for not being able to remember. I didn't say nothing about November, Jimmy. How did you know a colored girl was found out here in November 1936? Huh? How did you know that?"

He turned slowly to face her. She was coming toward him, shotgun raised.

"Say, now, there's no need for all this. You don't have to kill me. I'm different now. And look, you're all right. Come on, come on. You don't have to do this."

Hessie saw the sweat running down the side of his face. She watched as Jimmy started breathing heavy. His eyes darted around to see an escape, but there was none. She'd picked the right place for killin'.

"You set this up?" he asked.

"Yeah, Jimmy, I did. Me, that little colored girl from twelve years ago. The girl you raped and threw in a hole to die."

"Well, you shouldn't have tried to run."

He started to say more, but a shot rang out. Jimmy Pritchard was dead before he hit the ground.

The ride back was quiet. It was early morning when she got back to Ruth Ann's house.

Hessie handed her the key after she parked the truck. The front of Hessie's T-shirt was stained with dirt and sweat. A smudge of mud marked her cheek.

"You awright?" Ruth Ann looked her up and down.

Hessie cocked her head, listening. She nodded and walked down the steps into the misty morning. The only sound she heard was the birds beginning to awaken. No more shoveling. The grave was filled.

ABOUT THE EDITORS

RACHEL HOWZELL HALL is a *New York Times* bestselling author of seven novels, including *The Good Sister*, co-written with James Patterson, and the critically-acclaimed Detective Elouise Norton series. The *New York Times* called Lou Norton "a formidable fighter—someone you want on your side." Her newest novel, *They All Fall Down*, published in April 2019, pays homage to Agatha Christie's *And Then They Were None*. A featured writer on NPR's acclaimed "Crime in the City" series and the National Endowment for the Arts weekly podcast, Rachel has also served as a mentor in AWP's Writer to Writer Program and is currently on the board of directors of the Mystery Writers of America. She lives in Los Angeles with her husband and daughter.

Like her fictional character Claudia Rose, **SHEILA LOWE** is a real-life forensic handwriting expert who testifies in court cases. The mother of a tattoo artist and a former rock star, she lives in Ventura with Lexie the Evil Cat, where she writes the award-winning Forensic Handwriting series. Despite sharing living space with a cat, Sheila's mysteries are medium boiled, psychological suspense, definitely not cozy. She likes putting ordinary people into extraordinary circumstances and makes them squirm. Sheila has also published a series of non-fiction works about handwriting and personality.

LAURIE STEVENS is the author of the Gabriel McRay psychological thrillers. The book series has won twelve awards, among them the 2014 IPPY for Best Mystery/Thriller, *Library Journal's* Self-E Award, and Random House Editor's Book of the Month. Laurie is a hybrid author, both self-published and traditionally published. She is an active member of MWA, ITW, and a former board member of Sisters in Crime Los Angeles.

ABOUT THE CONTRIBUTORS

JULIE G. BEERS currently works as the PR & Creative Content Manager at Children's Burn Foundation. The non-profit works to prevent burns before they happen through educational programs and information, and helps child burn survivors heal and thrive. In her free time, Julie is a writer and editor with numerous credits. She has written for multiple television series including *Walker, Texas Ranger, Renegade,* and *Gene Roddenberry's Earth: Final Conflict.* This is Julie's third story to appear in a SinC/LA anthology. Her previous stories were included in the anthologies *LAst Exit to Murder* and *LAdies Night.*

JULIA BRICKLIN is the author of *Polly Pry: The Woman Who Wrote the West* (2018), and *America's Best Female Sharpshooter: The Rise and Fall of Lillian Frances Smith* (2017) and the upcoming true crime book *Blonde Rattlesnake: Burmah Adams, Tom White, and the 1933 Crime Spree that Terrorized Los Angeles* (2019). She has written numerous articles for academic journals and magazines. Bricklin grew up in southern California, obtained a journalism degree at Cal Poly San Luis Obispo and worked in the TV/film industry before obtaining her master's degree in history at Cal State Northridge. In addition to serving as associate editor of California History, the publication of the California Historical Society, she is a professor of history. She lives in Los Angeles with her husband and two children.

ROGER CANNON grew up in Downey, California, and has advanced degrees in French. Teaching tough, street-smart, Latino kids gave Roger rare access to the guarded subcultures of graffiti writers and gang kids, the basis for his debut novel, *Cross-Out.* The first sequel, *Fresh Pursuit,* is due late 2018. His philosophy is simple—pick a worthy target, keep moving forward, enjoy the ride. This has taken him to managing a World Champion baseball team, running with bulls in Pamplona, walking the entire Camino de Santiago, and writing decent books. Roger lives with his family in San Pedro.

TONY CHIARCHIARO has been writing fiction for the last twenty years, while raising a family and working full time. He is the author of a mystery/suspense novel, *The Most Likely Suspect* and is working on a sequel, *Murder on P Street*. Additionally, Tony has completed over a dozen short stories. He holds a Master's degree in Psychology and a law degree which helps him in understanding his characters as they work their way through the court system. He's been in an outstanding critique group for as long as he's been writing.

LISA CIARFELLA is a recent CSULB MFA graduate who writes dark tainted noir style prose, where bad people do bad things and not so bad people get caught up in the madness. Her writing's been featured on *Writers Who Kill, Near to the Knuckle*, Flash Fiction Offensive at *Out of the Gutter, Pulp-Metal Magazine, Ash-editcom, NoWastedInk*, and other places. She's thrilled to have "Tick-Tock" featured in the 2019 Sisters in Crime L.A. anthology and is busy cranking out more short stories and a first crime fiction novel, doggedly pursuing the game. For more on Lisa, drop by her blog *Ciarfella's Fiction Corner* at writingfictionnow.com, Facebook.com/lisajohnljc, or on Instagram at lisajohnljc-author.

CYNDRA GERNET wrote her first mystery story in 1957 as a sixth grader. To no one's surprise, it was not picked up for publication. She did not return to fiction writing until fifteen years ago when she signed up for a UCLA extension writing class. She continues to learn the craft of writing with gifted teacher and published author, Jerrilyn Farmer and the wonderful Friday morning writers' group.

Dr. **B.J. GRAF** lives in Los Angeles. Her story, "Shikata Ga Nai" was published in the Sisters in Crime anthology, *LAst Exit to Murder* (2013). *Genesys Rx*, her near-future-mystery novel, was shortlisted for the UCLA Kirkwood Writing Competition, and she has been working with Jerrilyn Farmer's masters' class. In addition to writing she is an Adjunct Professor who teaches Film Studies and Classical Mythology at Pepperdine University, UCLA, UCLA-Extension, and CSUN. Before teaching full time, she worked as V.P. of Development for Abilene Pictures. Her Ph.D. and M.A., both in Classics, are from Princeton University. Her B.A. is from Dartmouth College.

MARK HAGUE has made up stories (in writing) since forever, and has written short stories, novels, poetry, articles, newsletters, etc. and has had stories published in several anthologies.

A.P. JAMISON is a former banker who received her MFA from Columbia University in 2013. She is currently completing her first novel: *Securities & Insecurities*—a mystery set in an investment banking training program during the crazy cocaine and cash-fueled '80s where working on Wall Street really could be murder. She lives in California with her family and her neighbor's dog.

MICHEAL KELLY spent decades imprisoned in the dismal dungeons of software engineering. She made her escape and has never looked back. She is also a recovering art museum addict. Her fondest travel experience occurred when the staff of a tiny French museum closed the building for a long lunch, locking her inside. Rehabilitation is not proceeding as well as hoped.

ALISON MCMAHAN is an award-winning filmmaker and author. Her most recent film is *Bare Hands and Wooden Limbs* (2010), a documentary about a village of landmine survivors in Cambodia, narrated by Sam Waterston. Her historical mystery novel, *The Saffron Crocus* (2014), won the Rosemary Award for Best YA Historical in 2014 and the Florida Writers Association's Royal Palm Literary Award in 2015. Her short mystery "The New Score" appeared in the *Fish Out of Water Anthology*, and "The Drive By" in the *Busted* anthology, both April 2017, both nominated for Derringer Awards. "Kamikaze Iguanas" appeared in the MWA anthology for middle grade readers entitled *Scream and Scream Again*, edited by R.L. Stine, (2018). She is represented by Gina Panettieri of Talcott Notch Literary. AlisonMcMahan.com

PETER SEXTON is the award-winning author of *Shelter from the Storm*, and the upcoming detective thriller *Mercy Street*. He lives in Southern California with his son, Cameron. A life-long fan of the short story form, Sexton can often be found in his favorite coffee house penning a new short story freehand. He would like to dedicate "Darkness Keeps Chasing" to Lisa Lewis.

GOBIND TANAKA writes fiction, essays, and poetry. He belongs to SAG-AFTRA and Sisters in Crime. Two decades a technical writer, market researcher, and data analyst, in previous years Tanaka healed clients with acupressure and shiatsu. He taught yoga, meditation, Indian sword fighting, and Tai Chi. From a Marine veteran Tanaka learned combat handgun tactics and security consciousness. He believes wisdom and compassion are two sides of the same coin.

JENNIFER YOUNGER writes noir fiction. As a young girl, Jennifer often traveled to southern Virginia to visit relatives. Their conversations became the inspiration for her stories. As an adult, her curious nature has led her into back-alley Los Angeles joints with its pimps, gangsters and guns where she continues to explore the worlds her characters inhabit. When not thinking of ways her characters can bump off the bad guy or seduce a good one, Jennifer can be found voraciously reading all genres of fiction. She is a member of Mystery Writers of America, SoCal and Sisters in Crime, Los Angeles. She continues to seek out the dirty secrets of small Southern towns, similar to the ones in which her stories take place.

BOOKS

On the following pages are a few
more great titles from the
Down & Out Books publishing family.

For a complete list of books and to
sign up for our newsletter,
go to DownAndOutBooks.com.

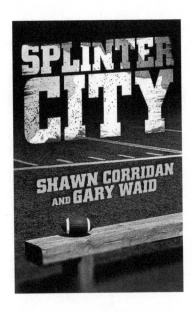

Splinter City
Shawn Corridan and Gary Waid

Down & Out Books
November 2018
978-1-948235-39-6

After nearly two decades in prison, high school gridiron great Dan Parrish returns to his hometown in rural Kansas with nothing more than a duffle bag and a desire to quietly get on with his life.

But picking up the pieces in a place where he was once revered isn't as easy as he hoped, especially for a convicted felon in the Bible Belt.

When Dan is offered a dream job—a coaching staff position with the Echo Junior College football team—he must decide between accepting the offer and risking his newfound freedom; or leaving Echo, tail between his legs, and breaking the promise he made to his dying father.

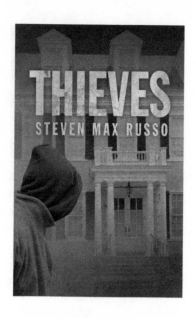

Thieves
Steven Max Russo

Down & Out Books
November 2018
978-1-948235-40-2

Dark, deadly and disturbing, *Thieves* will both horrify and delight you.

In his stunning debut thriller, Steven Max Russo teams a young cleaning girl with a psychopathic killer in a simple robbery that quickly escalates into a terrifying ordeal. Stuck in a deadly partnership, trapped by both circumstance and greed, a young girl is forced to play cat and mouse against her deadly partner in crime.

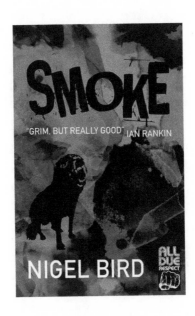

Smoke
Nigel Bird

All Due Respect, an imprint of
Down & Out Books
December 2018
978-1-64396-007-4

The Ramsay brothers are keen to move up in the world. They gather all their hopes in one basket and set up the Scottish Open dog-fighting tournament. In Leo they have the animal to win it.

Carlo Salvino returns home missing an arm and a leg. He's keen to win back the affections of his girlfriend and mother of his child. If he can take his revenge on the Ramsays, so much the better.

The Hooks, well they're just a maladjusted family caught up in the middle of it all.

Smoke: a tale of justice, injustice and misunderstanding.

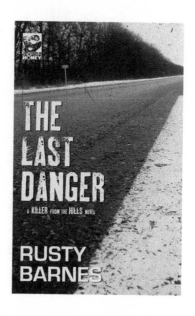

The Last Danger
A Killer from the Hills Novel
Rusty Barnes

Shotgun Honey, an imprint of
Down & Out Books
October 2018
978-1-64396-001-2

Three months after a shootout with the renegade Pittman family robbed him of his brother, Matt Rider is trying to put his life back together. His wounds are many, his sworn enemy Soldier Pittman may wake up and begin to tell what he knows, his wife is on the knife edge of sanity, and his teen daughter has gone missing with the son of his sworn enemy.

In a whirlwind series of killings, thefts and rash decisions, Rider ends up muling drugs across the Canadian border in order to save his daughter and wife from an even worse fate...

CPSIA information can be obtained
at www.ICGtesting.com
Printed in the USA
FSHW011820020319